Diego Marani

THE LAST
OF THE
VOSTYACHS

Translated by Judith Landry

Dedalus

Dedalus would like to thank Grants for the Arts in Manchester for its assistance in producing this book.

This book has been selected to receive financial assistance from English PEN's Writers in Translation programme supported by Bloomberg. English PEN exists to promote literature and its understanding, uphold writers' freedoms around the world, campaign against the persecution and imprisonment of writers for stating their views, and promote the friendly co-operation of writers and free exchange of ideas.
www.englishpen.org

Published in the UK by Dedalus Limited,
24-26, St Judith's Lane, Sawtry, Cambs, PE28 5XE
email: info@dedalusbooks.com
www.dedalusbooks.com

ISBN 978 1 907650 56 7

Dedalus is distributed in the USA by SCB Distributors,
15608 South New Century Drive, Gardena, CA 90248
email: info@scbdistributors.com   web: www.scbdistributors.com

Dedalus is distributed in Australia by Peribo Pty Ltd.
58, Beaumont Road, Mount Kuring-gai, N.S.W. 2080
email: info@peribo.com.au

First published by Dedalus in 2012
Copyright © 2002 Diego Marani
Published by arrangement with Marco Vigevani Agenzia Letteraria
Translation copyright © 2012 Judith Landry

The Author

Diego Marani was born in Ferrara in 1959. He is a policy officer of the European Commission in charge of the European multilingualism policy.

He is the inventor of the mock-European language Europanto in which he has been writing columns for newspapers and magazines all over Europe for many years. His collection of short stories in Europanto, *Las Adventures des Inspector Cabillot*, has been published by Dedalus.

He is the author of six novels including the highly acclaimed *New Finnish Grammar* and *The Last of the Vostyachs*. His most recent novel *Il Cane di Dio* will be published in Italy in 2012 and by Dedalus in 2013.

The Translator

Judith Landry was educated at Somerville College, Oxford where she obtained a first class honours degree in French and Italian. She combines a career as a translator of works of fiction, art and architecture with part-time teaching.

Her translations for Dedalus are: *New Finnish Grammar* and *The Last of the Vostyachs* by Diego Marani, *The House by the Medlar Tree* by Giovanni Verga, *The Devil in Love* by Jacques Cazotte, *Prague Noir: The Weeping Woman on the Streets of Prague* by Sylvie Germain and *Smarra & Trilby* by Charles Nodier.

To Simona, Alessandro and Elisabetta

"Jede Sprache ist ein Versuch"
(Every language is an experiment)
Wilhelm von Humboldt

I

They came out silently, without exchanging a glance; unhurriedly, expecting to be shot at any moment, to crumple on the spot, on to that mud they'd traipsed over so often. But now the camp was empty. The guards had all gone off during the night. The storeroom doors lay open, the chimneys of the barracks had ceased smoking. They fanned out from along the track dug out by the great wheels of the lorries, into the still dark forest, each in their own direction, without a word, as though in all those years spent locked up in there together they had never known each other. Ivan could still hear the odd thud, the sound of a broken branch, then nothing. So then he too pushed open the doors of the hut and went outside. A sooty mist hung over the wood, clinging to everything. The black wood of the huts, beaded with drops of grimy moisture, seemed to be sweating. Ivan hesitated to approach the main gate. He had never gone beyond it. For twenty years, getting up from his bench in the morning he had climbed straight on to the lorry, which then drove downhill behind the barracks, along the side of the mountain to the mine. But he'd never gone through the gates. He'd never seen them from the outside. He paused now to stare at them, and felt afraid. With one step he plunged backwards through time. A child was coming up towards him. He had a bow slung over his shoulder and was holding three dead squirrels by the tail. 'Another four and we'll be able to buy ourselves a bushel of flour down in the village,' thought Ivan as he looked at them. Then he set off down the track, slithering through mud up to his ankles. It was the end of summer, when the birds migrate, the bears go into hibernation and the first snow falls on the high meadows. But for Ivan it was a morning in spring. He spent the whole day walking, away from the mine, away from the Russians. He was still walking as a watery sun went down behind the trees. Sinking his feet into the moss, he stepped over the roots of service trees covered with pale berries, went through clouds of mosquitoes which settled on his face, then dissolved in a column of light inside the dense wood. Soon the white arctic night wiped away the shadows, the sky faded to a milky blur but Ivan carried on. He didn't stop until he saw the stumpy ridges of the Byrranga Mountains and breathed in the bitter scent of heather and sedge. He drank water from a puddle in the hollow of a rock and then at last allowed himself to stretch out exhausted on the ground, never taking his eyes off the familiar outline silhouetted in the distance. He saw the crest in the shape of a deer's head, and the two points which looked like a hare's ears. Hunting with his father, he had found those mysterious forms faintly disquieting. Though he could no longer see it, he could sense that the child was still there, running to and fro. Twenty years had gone by, but he had remained a child. He had waited for him.

Now Ivan could start again from that distant winter morning when the soldiers had arrived. They had urinated, laughing, on to the fire, on to the roasting meat, and Ivan had never forgotten that smell of scorched urine. They had taken all the furs: those of the otters, the beavers, the coot, even the wolverine which Ivan had found in his trap. They had pushed Ivan and his father into the lorry with their rifle-butts and taken them to the mine. Loading those stones into the wheelbarrow and washing them in the cold water, turning them over with a shovel, had been hard work. By the evening, Ivan could hardly move his hands. Trying not to think of food, he would sit huddled on the plank bed next to his father, listening to him singing his sad songs until he tumbled into sleep. He would dream about the mountains, the yurt in the middle of its clearing, his favourite animals. Strangely, he could see them from above, and suddenly he would realize that he was a falcon, flying above the trees, far from the darkness down below, the soldiers' boots, the mine. One night, without a word, his father suddenly pulled him down from the plank bed by the arm. Outside, the snow was chest-high and Ivan made his way through it with difficulty. There was no moon, no stars. The snow was dull, mud-flecked. All that could be heard in the freezing darkness was the rustling of their bodies as they sank into the snow. Someone gave a shout, nailed boots clumped down from the watchtowers, there was the sound of guns being loaded but the two shadows did not pause. Ivan's father carried on groping his way towards the wire fencing, thrusting his feet down into the snow with all his strength, holding his son firmly by the arm as he did so. Then two shots rang out in the darkness. He could see the soldiers' white breath in the torchlight. All around, dark shadows were looming up out of the snow, seeming to take an age to reach the runaways. Ivan felt hard hands grabbing him, hitting him on the face and in the stomach, then dragging him back into the hut. He climbed on to his plank bed and cowered there, gulping down mouthfuls of blood-streaked saliva. Shortly afterwards, several faceless men came to drag away his father by the feet. In the blue flash of their torches Ivan saw his head bouncing over the floor as though it had become detached from his body. By now it was a swollen lump of hair and mangled flesh. The soldiers were shrieking, thrusting their rifle butts at random through the ragged clothing into the bodies of the other prisoners as they lay on their plank beds. But no one moved, no one tried to fend them off. The blows sank into their shadowy forms, snapping bones, crushing flesh which seemed inert. At last the door clanged shut again, the padlocks could be heard grinding in the locks, the rasping voices of the soldiers faded into the distance, together with their heavy tread. Soon all was quiet again. Even the chinks of light between the boards faded from view. Then Ivan climbed down from his plank bed, aching all over, and felt his way towards his father on the floor. He clasped his ever colder hands, shook him, called out his name with such voice as he could muster, stroked his blood-spattered hair. Then he curled up, weeping, beside the lifeless body, sought out its mouth gently with his fingers and pressed his lips against it, hoping to replace its vanished life with his own warm breath. He spent the whole night pressed up against that cold, hard body which no longer spoke to him.

Since that day, Ivan had not uttered a word. He had carried on washing stones in the pool of icy water, had split rocks with his pick-axe, had pushed the wheelbarrow along the steep, slippery path, had gone about all his work with lowered eyes, had endured all manner of humiliation, eating without looking to see what they poured into his mess tin, getting up at dawn and going to bed at sunset without a word. The new convicts who arrived in the camp thought that Ivan was dumb. Only the ones who'd been there longer knew why he never spoke. The soldiers too – even the ones who had killed his father – had forgotten. They didn't recognize him among the crowd of tattered death's-heads they prodded into the lorries every day. When Ivan became a man, no one in the mine any longer had any idea who that short, sinewy local was, with his flat face and jutting Tartar cheekbones. Everyone who knew his story was long dead. The others felt alarmed by that inexplicable silence which seemed akin to madness. The cover of his file, kept in a cupboard in the barracks, bore just one word: Ivan.

14

All it contained were a few crumpled pages concerning his arrest for poaching.

Ivan broke off a branch and swung it round his head to drive off the mosquitoes and the bad memories. Now he had other things to think worry about. He had to take care of the child. First of all he had to teach him how to bend a birch branch into a bow, how to braid and stretch the fibres of the bark to make ropes, how to cut an arrow so that it would imitate the falcon's cry. Soon he would have to get by on his own and spend the winter in the forest. He would sleep in huts covered with skins and bark. He would dig into the frozen water of the lakes for bait. A thick row of young birch trees growing by the banks of a pool caught Ivan's eye. He walked out over the sand and caught sight of the odd fish darting through the still water. He bent one of the saplings towards him, broke off a gleaming white branch and turned it around in his hands, exclaiming aloud: 'This will make a splendid bow.' Then salmon rose to the surface, dozens of coot flew skywards from their hiding-places among the reeds, thousands of hamsters emerged from their burrows and dived blindly into the muddy marshes; in the distant tundra, whole droves of wild reindeer galloped off in alarm. The lake waters puckered beneath a breath of wind, which then ran like a shiver throughout the forest. The mist melted away and the sun glittered on the tree trunks. It was twenty years since Ivan had uttered a word, twenty years since the language spoken by the oldest tribe of the Proto-Uralic family, the Vostyachs – cousins of the Samoyeds, the wild bear-hunters who once lived in the Byrranga Mountains and whom scientists believed to be extinct – had been heard anywhere in Northern Siberia. Hearing those sounds, all nature quaked. Things that had not been named for years emerged sluggishly from their long sleep, realizing they still existed. Each animal in turn answered Ivan's words with its own call. They were back – the men who could talk with wolves, who knew the names of the black fish hidden in the mud of the Arctic lakes, of the fleshy mosses which, for just a few summer's days, purpled the rocks beneath the Tajmyr Peninsula; the men who had found the way out of the dark forests into another world but never the way back.

For the first few days, Ivan wandered through the thick of the trees and over the rocks, prompted by clues from his eyes and ears. For the first time in years, his heart felt untroubled. But he missed his fellow-men. He was looking for his people, because now at last he wanted, he needed to speak. He remembered the faces around the fire, the snow-covered hunters, dressed in skins, crowding into the yurt. They would sit down around the embers, drink a bowl of curdled milk and then sink into a deep sleep. When they came down from the mountains in the spring, their gaze was as piercing as that of the animals they had hunted throughout the winter. Ivan called out names which had come back to him the moment he opened his mouth to utter them. Korak, Häinö, Taypok. No one answered, no one came forward to meet the returning convict. He followed ancient paths scoured out in the rock, sometimes he came upon the skeleton of a burned-out yurt, or strips of hardened leather hanging from some branch. But he did not meet a living soul. Only the distant wolves answered his call. The whole forest was one vast graveyard without graves. His people were buried beneath the black earth where moss and mushrooms grew. They had dissolved into the rotting mud that lay at the bottom of the pools, into the dark flesh of the berries, into the sickly sap of the birch trees, swayed by mysterious gusts of wind.

Ivan had realized that the child who sometimes followed him, then disappeared again between the ferns, was not alive. He was a vision, a spirit without a home; a dead thing rejected by the world to come. A silent shade. Yet, in his desire to break out of his solitude, Ivan had begun to talk to him. He told him stories he did not know he knew, but which came into his head with every step he took in those familiar places. To his surprise, he also found himself singing, remembering the sound of instruments which did not seem to be part of any known memory, but which beat in his temples the moment he began to sing. One after the other, he rediscovered the hidden paths he had taken with his father, he recognized the copse of black birches where the young deer, their antlers still soft and pulpy as young bark, would go to hide. He found the waterfall in the mountain stream he'd gone to with his father to catch salmon, from which you could see the distant outline of the far-off peaks, those furthest to the north, the first to catch the snow. He came to the bare, dry upland plain, where all that grew was the odd dwarf birch tree, clinging to the rock, the odd reddish dwarf pine, laid low by frost. He followed the stony track up as far as he could and, though he could not see it, he knew that somewhere, far below him, lay the sea. With his white bow he hunted and killed animals whose flesh he had no intention of eating: what he craved was their strong, sour smell. Greedily, he breathed in the smell of lives which were being cut short in order to quicken his own, which was still in suspended animation. What most alarmed him, in the new world he was discovering, was its silence. It was too similar to that of the nights in the hut, when he'd been in the mine. So Ivan made himself a drum out of reindeer skin. He remembered his father's skilful hands as he bound strips of leather around the carefully shaped piece of spruce. He would play it in front of the fire on moonless nights, when it was dangerous to fall asleep and you might be plummeted into the world of the dead. This was what had happened to old Kunnas one October night in his hut when he was getting ready to go out hunting. The wind had crept down quietly from the Byrranga Mountains, slipped into the forest almost at ground level, without setting the branches stirring. It had stolen into the huts, whistling among the skins, among the sheets of bark, and had frozen the blood of all the sleepers in their veins. Kunnas had been found seated on his rush mat, his bow clutched in his hand and his quiver slung over his shoulder. His eyes were open; he seemed surprised to have been taken by death so mindlessly.

At sunrise Ivan would tie his drum around his waist and follow the stony track up to the topmost point. Then he would kneel down on the highest rock and start to play, to tell the world that he was still alive. He rapped on the taut skin with both his hands, with the bones of animals, and, as he did so, his arms and fingers remembered movements they had made earlier in another life.

The first snowfall came towards the end of autumn. Ivan chose a sheltered spot in the wood and built himself a yurt of animal skins. Now, at night, he could hear the wolves coming closer and closer; in the darkness, he saw their yellow eyes. Then he would fashion arrows, which would then be heated in the fire, and talk to the wolves aloud, to scare them off. But they stayed motionless behind the trees, fixing their gaze on man and fire alike, pricking their ears when Ivan doused the flames. Then they would curl up until dawn, when he would see them move off into the misty forest. One night Ivan had a disturbing dream. Awaking with a start, he heard the wolves howling; they were all around his yurt. Dozens of wolves were staring at him, lifting their muzzles skywards and baying piteously. Then Ivan understood. They were his people. Fleeing the soldiers, the men of his tribe had hidden in deep underground lairs in the mountain caves. They had become wolves themselves, and now they lived in the forests. That was why they were seeking him out now. He must call them back, sing and play to them to bring them back into the world of men. So each night Ivan would play his drum for them. He would light the fire and wait until the stars that made up Orion were above him in the sky – the glinting iron belt, the drawn bow and glowing arrow, pointing at the darkness. Then he would tap his fingers gently on the drum and look towards the wood. The wolves would narrow their eyes and whimper uneasily, scenting fire. Then they would circle in and sit on their hind quarters until the stars faded from the sky. But none of them ever took on human form. They had been too long out of the world of men, they had ventured too far among the beasts, and the way back was lost. Ivan would have to go right deep into their lairs and bring them back one by one.

At first, Ivan had felt wary of the fair-haired woman he'd come upon in the village inn, who seemed so eager to hear him talk. Her eyes were not unkind, she wasn't wearing a military uniform, her voice was pleasant and she spoke the language of the turnip-growers. But Ivan sensed a hint of Russian in her accent, and he was also wary of the strange contraption she always had with her, and into which she would ask him to speak. He was afraid it was a trap to lure him away from his mountains and have him locked up in the mine again.

At the beginning of winter Ivan had discovered the village where the turnip-growers lived; it stood at the edge of the forest, in the direction of the great river, but he had never ventured into it. Its houses, with their tarred roofs, reminded him too much of the barracks in the mine. He stayed hidden in the trees, observing it from afar: its smoking chimneys and its inn, where the lorries from the saw-mill would draw up, laden with timber. He would observe the bluish strip of road as it wound its way into the distance, afraid that columns of shrieking soldiers might come into view from one moment to the next. But nothing at all emerged from the tundra. The colour of the sky changed, the wood gave out new scents, and it began to snow hard on the Byrranga Mountains. A blizzard raged over the forests and newly frozen lakes for days on end. The wind piled the heavy snow into scaly dunes which shifted daily, so that the landscape of the tundra was always subtly changing. It was dry snow, too powdery to walk on, even with snow-shoes. Ivan couldn't get to his traps, nor indeed go hunting. Low, thorny bushes were all that grew on the upland plain; it had now become a shifting desert, and Ivan had completely lost his bearings. The two points which looked like a hare's ears and a deer's head were cloaked in persistent cloud. Such powdery snow did not bode well; it meant that the winter had started off on a bad footing. Ivan remembered that the old people in the village would talk of a far-off time when the scourge of this powdery snow first struck. The tundra was treacherous, the marshes impassable. At the least cold times of day, gaps would form in the ice on the lakes and the reindeer would plunge into the freezing water. Within a few minutes they would have died a silent death; they would thrash around, baring their teeth, until they were numbed by the cold. At night the ice would close up again, transforming their carcasses into so many gruesome statues. The Vostyachs couldn't go hunting for weeks on end. The snow was like sand, some six feet deep, and walking on it might end in suffocation. Nothing was possible without snow-shoes, but hunters were slowed down with such contraptions on their feet, and by the time they had drawn their bows their prey had fled. Children whimpered with hunger, and mothers often woke up in the morning to find them dead in their arms. The old people would slink out of the village unobserved. They would go off to die, burying themselves in the snow so as not to be a burden on their families. Men ate the drum-skins, the bark of trees, such roots as had managed to push their way through the frozen ground. As they became increasingly weak, many lacked even the strength to dig or to collect firewood, and their fires went out. By now there was no coming and going around the yurts, and smoke meant that death had paid a call. Then, one night, the wind changed and the stars reappeared in the sky. The dry, powdery snow crusted over and the wood creaked ominously, as though each trunk were being wrenched apart. When the sun rose, the whole forest was strewn with reindeer, elk and deer, trapped up to the chest in the ice. Exhausted by their recent hardships, the men of the village dragged themselves out to where the creatures lay. They cut their throats and lay down in the snow to drink the warm blood as it spurted out.

That was what the old men said, and Ivan was afraid of the powdery snow which could spell death.

So he decided to go down to the village where the turnip-growers lived, to exchange the odd fur for a bit of bread and dried meat. But when he pushed open the door of the inn, he was greeted by hostile stares. Ivan ran his eyes over the group to assure himself that they were not soldiers. He took off his fur hat and greeted them with a nod. Then he laid his skins on the table and asked those present to name their price. But no one said a word; they merely inspected him in stony silence. They had stopped drinking and playing cards; the only sound was the crackling of the stove and the innkeeper's wife rinsing out a pan in the kitchen behind the counter. It was then that the fair-haired young woman had come in. She had been kind, she'd had someone bring him some soup and had bought all the squirrels' tails. The woodsmen had gone back to their drinking and card games, and the hum of their conversation once more mingled with the cigarette smoke and the smell of cabbage and wood smoke. But when the woman turned on the strange contraption which registered your voice, Ivan had taken fright. He had picked up his skins, gone out of the inn and taken refuge in the woods. That night he hadn't slept in his hut, but in a hole he'd hollowed out of the snow. In the days that followed, armed with his bow, he had again gone to the edge of the forest to observe the inn. He was afraid that the fair-haired woman might have gone to get the soldiers. But nothing in the village seemed to have changed. The chimneys carried on smoking above the tarred roofs and the battered lorries from the sawmill juddered along the icy road, scattering long trails of sawdust as they went. One morning, climbing on to the ridge of snow which was his lookout post, Ivan heard the woman calling him. Then he caught sight of her in the snowy meadow behind the inn. She had her hands around her mouth and was calling towards him, in Vostyach:

'*Vostyach! Rony noxeita pedeya!*'

Ivan still had a good stock of squirrels' tails. The woman had been kind to him. She had given him bread and had not called the soldiers. So he left his hiding-place and went towards her.

From that day onwards Ivan started to go down to the inn and speak into the little black box the woman placed before him. He would get the best squirrels' tails down from the walls of his yurt and take them to her. On sunny days he would go into the wood with her and call out the names of all the plants and animals they came upon as they walked. The woman would write them carefully in a notebook the same colour as the one belonging to the doctor who came each summer to inspect the barracks in the mine and who would scatter white lime over the plank beds. Ivan felt pleased as the pages gradually filled up. By now he was proud of all the words he knew. He felt as though he were the owner of a personal treasure-trove. He carried on for as long as they continued to come into his mind, even adding some invented ones of his own, to please the fair-haired young woman who listened to him smilingly. He was saddened when he realized that his knowledge had been exhausted, that he couldn't tell her the names of the things that were in the inn, nor the instruments used by the woodcutter in his hut with its corrugated iron roof. But then, gradually, the young woman herself started to talk his language. Ivan did not know all the words she used, but he understood many of them all the same; it was as if he had known them for ever. They prompted him to remember others, which he would shout out loudly, as though he had been groping for them for years, and it was only then that they had come back into his mind. With more words at his disposal, Ivan could tell the woman many more things. He told her about the mine, about his father being murdered by the soldiers, about fishing for whitefish in the lake, about the yurt encampment which he had been unable to find when he returned to the Byrranga Mountains. He told her how deer is hunted, how its flesh is dried, how to build traps for wolverines. The fair-haired woman was surprised to learn that Ivan did not skin beavers, but would roast them by tossing them, gutted, into the burning coals. That seemed to set her thinking, and she dashed off several pages in her notebook. Ivan was happy at last to be able to tell someone about the minutiae of his days. Only now that someone knew he was alive, and was able to talk to him, did he feel truly free, reborn to a new life where the mine had never existed. He was sure that sooner or later his people too would return to life, would emerge from the wolves' lairs and begin to talk. Sooner or later, Korak, Häinö and Taypok would come back to hunt with him.

This was the only subject he never succeeded in explaining to his new friend. The woman seemed to understand everything Ivan told her. She would nod and write, copy down the words she heard, dividing them up by subject. But when Ivan tried to explain to her about the other Vostyachs who had become wolves, she would shake her head and was clearly mystified:

'*Tyonya? Miwa tyonya*?' she would ask, frowning.

She would draw a wolf in the notebook, make a circle around it and hand the pencil to Ivan, who would make deep marks on the white paper, then go over them with his fingertips.

Ivan felt strangely peaceful in her presence. Sometimes her affectionate face would appear to him in dreams of when he'd been a child, living in the yurt. But then she had a different smile, and a more fragile look, which somehow frightened him. She looked like the cork masks hanging from the walls. On snowy afternoons, while she was going through her notes, seated at a table in the inn – which would be empty, except for the odd snoozing drunkard, propped up against the wall – Ivan would settle down on a skin next to the stove, and wait for her to finish. He listened to the crackle of the flames, the sounds of her writing and rubbing out, the whirring of the black box as it unleashed his words into the empty room, exactly as he had spoken them to her. Only in her presence would he feel his muscles relax, feel again that melting sense of utter security which he had had as a child, curled up in front of the fire, watching his father making arrows for hunting coot. The fair-haired woman was deeply engrossed in her writing, sometimes pausing to gaze into the empty air. But every so often she would also cast a glance in Ivan's direction, a look so tender and protective that it almost hurt, from which he could not look away. That unknown woman was the only being in the world who wished him well, who, by calling him by name, also caused him to exist. As he did with his wolves. Ivan sensed this, and it amazed him. He explored the feeling in his heart, both fascinated and horrified at the knowledge that one day it would be taken from him.

Professor Jaarmo Aurtova crossed the floor of his study, making the parquet creak. He stopped in front of his desk, between the portrait of Marshal Mannerheim in full-dress uniform and an old map by the Arab geographer Ibn Al-Idrisi. He cleared his throat, lifted his chin and embarked, not for the first time, on the concluding speech he was to deliver at the XXIst Congress of Finno-Ugric, trying to keep his eyes from the typescript he was holding in his hand.

'My warmest and most respectful greetings to you all –to the minister, the rector, the mayor, to my distinguished colleagues, my illustrious guests, ladies and gentlemen. It is a great honour for me to present my report to this XXIst congress of Finno-Ugric languages which, after so many years, is finally being held here in Helsinki. Essentially, our city is the capital of the Finno-Ugric World, the symbol of the political and economic success of this culture of ours which has for too long remained unjustly little known. It is Finland which has brought homo finnicus *into Europe, no longer as a slave but as a free citizen. Furthermore, the arrival in Finland of such an illustrious body of scientists is confirmation of the high standard of our university research and our country's dominant position in a science which has always been particularly dear to us – perhaps more so than to any of our linguistic cousins. Now at least we are no longer alone in this corner of Europe, because Estonian is at last being spoken and taught again in Tallinn.*

And every Fino-Ugric language which is saved from extinction is tantamount to a promise of eternity for our whole culture.

(Probable applause), his secretary had written in brackets in the margin, marking the spot with an asterisk.

It's true that we are glad that the Gulf of Finland is there to separate us from our Estonian friends and shield us from all their "tuds" and "tabs'. But perhaps with time, as we get to know each other better, we shall at least be able to convince them that "stopp" can also be written with one "p", without in any way dishonouring the rule of the doubled consonant!

(Wait for probable end of laughter), also in brackets, also with an asterisk.

As we shall see over the course of the next three days, the study of Finno-Ugric languages has made great progress over recent years. The opening of frontiers that were once impassable, together with great advances in science, has enabled us to know more and more about our languages and the history of the peoples who speak them. Today, it is increasingly clear that the Ugro-Finns were by no means a pack of hunter-gatherers lacking in all civilization, as one school of thought continues to maintain, against all the evidence. As early as the Bronze Age, the Ugro-Finns had reached a level of development equivalent, if not superior, to that of the Mediterranean peoples. They practised advanced forms of agriculture and cattle-rearing. Furthermore, as we now know, thanks to the much milder climate of the time, our ancestors were also able to cultivate the vine. Who knows, had it not been for the glaciation of the Neolithic Period, today the finest "millesimes" might be maturing in the cellars of Uusimaa, and Laplanders might be quaffing champagne. So, long live the greenhouse effect! With good use of our saunas we could heat the entire planet! In a hundred years, what today is regarded as the chilly outer edge of Europe might be transformed into the garden of Eden, and our language might have become what it should rightfully always have been: the Latin of the Baltic!

(Further laughter and applause), as suggested by an asterisk.

As to the question of our earliest ethnic origins, recent studies have been conclusive. Faced with new evidence, even our Russian colleagues will be obliged to think again in connection with a well-established falsehood to which they have clung desperately over the years, and which has been made use of by an ideology which died away much more speedily than our languages: for what was once mere supposition is now a certainty. Recent archaeological discoveries in Ingria and Scania, corroborated by carbon 14 dating, confirm that the Ugro-Finnic civilization did indeed develop beyond the Urals, but they also prove that it migrated towards Europe very early on, reaching the lands where it is found today at the same period as the Indo-European peoples, and many centuries before the Slavs. So that the alleged kinship between the Ugro-Finnic and the Ural-Altaic branches, from which the Mongols and Eskimos descend, is to be excluded once and for all. The so-called Eskimo-Aleutian hypothesis has been proved to be baseless. Recent discoveries in this field prove that the Uralic linguistic melting-pot was more extensive than had originally been thought, and indeed cast doubt upon the very concept of Indo-European languages. Indo-Europeans should more properly be referred to as Indo-Iranians, and it is they who are the true Asiatics of Europe, not us. Right from the dawn of history we have belonged geographically to the continent of Europe, indeed we might say that we are the first Europeans, we, the Finnic peoples, and that Finnish is Europe's oldest language!'

Whenever he reached this part of the speech, Aurtova would always become flustered. He would imagine the inscrutable faces of the Russian linguists, that of Juknov in particular, always in the front row, dressed in black, the headphones with the simultaneous translation clapped firmly to his ears, his unforgiving gaze obscured behind his glasses. Then he would see Olga Pavlovna's mocking smile, her know-it-all expression. He knew that she would enjoy discomfiting him by quoting his old articles, written with her when she was still an unknown researcher, burning with idealism. This made him jumpy, he would start to strike the wrong tone, mumbling his words, rather than pronouncing them clearly, one by one, in expectation of the effect they would have on the wizened faces of his adversaries.

Professor Aurtova turned off the lamp, stuffed his typescript into a drawer and struck a match to light the table-candlestick. He liked the smell of wax, the flickering of the candles in the darkness. He slipped a hand behind the big Finnish dictionary and pulled out a bottle of cognac and a crystal glass. He poured himself a drink and walked over to the large French window. Below, the cathedral square was covered with snow, the street lamps were all lit and the windows of the houses were festooned with strips of little lights. The trams slid by noiselessly, sending out showers of blue sparks. It was the harshest winter for decades. The temperature had gone down to minus 30, and the whole bay of Helsinki was frozen up, all the way out as far as the lighthouse at Harmaja. This year perhaps we might be able to go on foot all the way to Tallinn, he thought to himself. He enjoyed the feel of the biting air as it whipped his face, the grandiose vista of his city, the white vastness that lit up the northern night. Snow always has a sense of wildness about it, and the footsteps of the passers-by on the flight of steps outside the cathedral gave the professor a pleasing feeling of mystery, as though they were unknown spoors met with in some wild wood.

He took a sip of cognac, and felt a welcome shudder at the instant burst of warmth which ran through his veins. Then came a sudden knock at the door, and his secretary entered the room.

'You didn't collect your post, professor,' she said, putting an envelope down on the table.

'I completely forgot!' he said, lifting a hand to his forehead.

'If there's nothing else, I'd quite like to be off...'

She lingered on the threshold, peering owlishly at Aurtova from behind her thick glasses.

'Of course, Leena, go by all means. And have a quiet day tomorrow, because from Sunday it'll be all work and no play.' He moved back to the table without closing the window.

'Yes indeed... Goodnight, professor,' she said, retreating from the cold.

The envelope contained just one letter. It had a Russian stamp, and the address was written by hand. He recognized the writing.

Dear Jarmo,

I'm passing through Moscow and I'm sending you this letter so that I can be the first to give you a sensational bit of news. I've just spent a few months with the Nenets and Nganasan, making recordings of local speakers. As you know, my passion has always been the northern Samoyedic languages, so I paid another visit to those parts on the track of some minor dialect to record before it died out. Over the last few

years I really think I've catalogued them all! At the end of
November I found myself in a remote village in the Tajmyr
peninsula. I was waiting for the weather to improve so that
I could get to Norilsk, where I was to take the plane to Saint
Petersburg, but I was left stranded by a blizzard, so I had to
resign myself to a long wait. I spent my days copying out my
notes in a dismal room in the only inn, when one afternoon
my guide came into my room in a state of high excitement.
He knows I speak Nganasan, so he never addresses me in
Russian. But I have difficulty in understanding him when he
talks in that Polustrov dialect of his, so I went off with him
somewhat unwillingly, not really knowing what he wanted.
He took me to the floor below, the bar-room I suppose you
could call it, which was strangely lively for the time of day.
And there, surrounded by a muttering crowd, was a truly
weird individual. Physically, he looked like an Inuit, but more
athletic, and darker-complexioned. He was entirely dressed in
skins, had a bow slung over his shoulder and was holding a
string of squirrels' tails. At his feet was a sack of skins. When
they saw me come in, everyone stopped muttering. The guide
pointed at the man and whispered in my ear, in Russian: 'We
can't understand a word of anything he says!' I went up to him
and tried addressing him in Vogul, thinking he might belong
to some Eastern Ugric tribe. He listened to me carefully, but
then frowned in puzzlement. Yet I noticed that those sounds
were familiar to him, even if he didn't understand them. He
looked at me questioningly, waving the string of squirrels'
tails. He put them on the table and began unstringing them,
so that I could see them better. He must have already repeated
himself several times without making himself understood. At
first I could understand nothing: just a blurred flow of Uralic
sounds. I thought it was some Dolgan dialect which had

eluded me, and I was almost irritated at the thought of having to deal with yet another one. I didn't even feel like going back up to my room and fetching my tape recorder. But the more he talked, the more I realized that this was another language entirely. It might be some localized variant of Jurak, but I was unconvinced by the *coup de glotte*. At first it was the *schwa* which unsettled me: I'd never heard it so unvoiced before. Nganasan has one that is very similar; but when I noticed how the man pronounced his velar affricatives and above all his retroflex palatals, I was no longer in any doubt: the man I was listening to was a Vostyach!

Dear Jarmo, you can imagine how I felt. I immediately rushed upstairs to get my tape recorder and encouraged the man to talk into it. And I could hardly believe my ears. They're all there, the consonants which mark the transition between the Finnic languages and the Eskimo-Aleut ones. Even the fricative lateral with the labiovelar appendix! I haven't finished mapping the phonetic analogies, but will have done so in time for the conference, even if I have to work on my new paper round the clock. So, goodbye Samoyedic dialects, hallo Vostyach! If you wanted the Helsinki conference to be a turning point in the study of the Finno-Ugric languages, your wish is granted. Now at last we can be certain that, in antiquity, languages belonging to the same family were spoken from the Baltic to the great plains of North America. Who knows, Jarmo, perhaps your ancestors included some Sioux chief who fought at Little Big Horn! In a word, you can see that the Eskimo-Aleutian theory was indeed correct, and that it is not just because they speak an agglutinitive language that the Inuit have a vowel harmony similar to that of you and your Finns. The Vostyach says his name is Ivan. But when he talks of himself he describes himself as "vostyach", which means "man". So for the people of the village he has become Ivan Vostyach. He's probably a survivor from some gulag. At the inn they told me that there was a large mining settlement on the far side of the lakes, an open-cast mine where they sent convicts to break stones and wash them by the ton, all to extract a few specks of gold. Hell on earth, apparently. When wages stopped arriving from Moscow, the overseers did a bunk and the few remaining prisoners escaped.

My Vostyach understands Nganasan: perhaps someone spoke it at the mine. He also understands a little Russian, but he can't speak a word. It's a language which frightens him: as soon as he hears it, he tenses up and looks away. It probably has the most terrible associations for him. So at first we communicated by gesture, or in rudimentary Nganasan. But then I started learning Vostyach, and it wasn't long before I could compose the odd sentence. Mostly, I myself reconstructed the words, basing myself on those I heard him pronounce. But it worked, and Ivan understood me. At first he was disconcerted on hearing me speak his language. But then something within him seemed to melt, and we immediately became friends. To begin with I couldn't persuade him to stay in the village for more than a few hours. He seemed nervous when he came into the inn, and even when he accepted a bowl of soup he was continually looking out of the window, peering anxiously along the grey road which wound up into the steppe, on the lookout for soldiers. But I felt that he sought me out, that he liked being with me. Every time he heard his language issuing from my mouth, he seemed enchanted. Uttering those primitive sounds, I too felt that I was back in the distant past. It's true that you can have the illusion that you know all about a people by reading about their civilization in libraries – about their kings, their battles, their religion. But until you take possession of their language, you really know nothing of them. Ivan wanted to speak, he was hungry for words and company. Loneliness and fear had marked him physically as well as mentally. He moved furtively, like an animal lying in wait; he pricked up his ears at noises I myself could not hear, and when he was worried he would show his unease by clenching and unclenching his fists. I've never seen such misshapen hands. His fingers were just stubby protuberances, without nails, the skin on them was tough and hairless. Ivan would always return to the forest before dark. He'd stay away for a couple of days and then reappear in the village bringing me some squirrels' tails. He said he couldn't stay for very long, he had to get back to his people. I had imagined a whole tribe of Vostyachs up there in the woods. But then I saw that he must be referring to something else – his animals, perhaps, or the spirits of his ancestors. He always had that strange sack of skins on his shoulder. He never opened it in my presence and he never put it down. One afternoon when he had fallen asleep on the inn floor, I looked inside it, to find it contained a few stones, some animal bones, feathers, bears' teeth and little braids of hair. When he woke up, it was the first thing he reached for. It was already beginning to get dark, but he set off anyway towards the woods at quite a pace, as though there really were someone waiting for him up there. It was hard to know where he lived, because it was impossible to follow him: as soon as he entered the wood he was immediately lost from view. The snow seemed to close in after him. But, over time, I managed to gain his confidence. He realized that not all Russians were bad, even if on the few occasions when he did stay on in the village he would sleep in some shed, or in the outhouses of the sawmill, rather than be near other human beings. There was a distant land, I told him, where there were many people who would like to get to know him: not Russians, but people of his own race, who spoke a language similar to his own. I explained to him that he was not alone, but that he belonged to a large and ancient tribe who were his brothers, and who would be eager to meet him. He was very struck by my talk of this great tribe, and questioned me closely about it. So finally I persuaded him to come with me to Helsinki. But I had to reassure him that there are no Russians there.

I stayed on in the Tajmyr Peninsula for a few more weeks and made a complete catalogue of all the words he knew. Unfortunately, his vocabulary is very limited. But, thanks to certain roots, I managed to construct a number of etymological hypotheses, though of course they are yet to be proved correct. Hunting for words became our game. We'd go around the forest and Ivan would put a name in Vostyach to everything he saw. Whenever he remembered this or that word, the name of some tree or object, he was triumphant. He knew he was making me happy and would coming running towards me, wreathed in smiles. He offered me his words like gifts. He must have suffered a great deal, and I sensed that the aftermath of such suffering still weighed upon him. Sometimes his mood would darken for no apparent reason, as though he were dogged by frightening images which he could not shake off. Then he would run off into the woods alone. At times I felt as though I were dealing with a child, he is so vulnerable, so naïve, so incapable of applying any form of reason to certain aspects of everyday life. Yet he knows how to make bows and arrows, dress hides and set traps. In the deepest woods he can find his bearings like a human compass. He can smell distant scents on the air and follow them. But his intelligence seems somehow one-dimensional. He moves in just one direction, among the things he knows. He makes no distinction between reality and fantasy. When he does not understand something, he instantly takes fright.

On the morning of our departure, after so much snow, a chilly sun appeared and the forest was tinged with pink. Waiting for the local bus which was to take us to Norilsk, looking out through the inn window, I gazed in awe at the forms of the snow-laden trees. The innkeeper's wife had just lit the stove, and the scent of resin wafted through the room. The big pot of water for the soup had just begun to boil, and the steam was causing the panes gradually to mist over. Everything felt strangely blank, slow-moving, suffused with sadness. Seated on the ground, Ivan was gazing raptly out at the dazzling light. Together with his sack of skins, he had brought with him a drum made of reindeer hide, which he kept clutched to his chest, his fingers spread out over it. I went up to him and sat beside him. I told him that the inn was not my home, but that I lived in a distant city, and that after our trip to Helsinki I would not be coming back with him to the forests of the Tajmyr Peninsula. He gave me a bewildered look. He stared angrily at my suitcase, inspected my city outfit – so different from my normal shabby village wear – with disapproval. He shook his head, retreating as though he didn't want to hear me. I tried to reassure him, telling him I'd be back to see him from time to time. He promised me that if I was leaving him because he couldn't provide me with any new words, he would get the wolves to tell him some. They knew many more than he, but he would have to persuade them to speak to him again, he said, looking sadly out towards the forest. He sighed. He clearly wanted to ask me something, but did not have the words. He made a vague gesture, then gave up, crestfallen. He was trying to understand how far I would be from his mountains, mentally measuring distances which for him were unimaginable. I went up to the misty windows and drew a rough map of Russia, in the form of a circle, on which I made two dots. One was Saint Petersburg, the other the Tajmyr Peninsula, as I explained to him. Ivan came up to me to look more closely, then rubbed his hand angrily over the pane. He ran to the next window, and the next, wiping away the condensation. Then he went to the back of the room and stared out at me from the semi-darkness; although I could not see him, I knew that he was crying. Then he put on his jacket, picked up his sack and drum and left the room. I was afraid that he would do his usual disappearing trick, and that I'd never see him again. On this occasion, though, he allowed me to follow him out to the wood. He stopped on a small rise and arranged his drum carefully on his chest. I knew that he did not like to be observed when he was playing, so I went to stand behind a tree. I saw him crouch down in the snow, put his hand in his sack and draw out a mask made of birch bark, which he then put on. Until that point, I'd never noticed it among his possessions. He stayed crouched there without moving for some time, then began to beat slowly, intensely and increasingly loudly on the drum-skin. It was as though he were embarking on a fight, as though with that incessant, insistent beat he might rid the world of disharmony and give it the steady rhythm of his own music. I felt as though all living matter were now moving to the rhythm of his drumbeat, breathing in time to it; falling seamlessly into step with him, walking beside him – only to plummet once more into its normal, fatal disarray. He was singing words I'd never heard him use. His voice was different now – deep and somehow majestic. He articulated each sound cautiously, as though he were almost afraid of it, as though it might unleash something uncontrollable, superhuman. He turned his head from side to side as he proceeded with his awesome dance, twisting his neck so far in each direction that I felt that I might see his head wrenched from his body and fall with a thud on to the snowy ground. There was pain in his voice, a sense of irreparable solitude, like a maze of ice settling into new and ever more intricate, tunnel-like formations as his song proceeded. Jarmo, I felt as furtive as a thief, hidden among those trees. For a moment I thought that it would be better to leave Ivan Vostyach there where he was, in his own land; that introducing him to people so different from himself would cause him suffering, make him feel even more alone. What did he know about Finno-Ugric or Proto-Uralian? What did it matter to him that he was the last of the Vostyachs? I suddenly felt that I was being purely selfish, going around with my tape recorder on the trail of dialects as though they were so many fur-bearing animals, pillaging memories in order to stuff them and put them on show in dismal museums. I thought of all those dazed little old men I'd gone to torment with my microphone, forcing them to remember things they might well have preferred to forget. I expected them to unroll the grief of a lifetime for my sole benefit. But even they were less vulnerable than Ivan Vostyach: they had houses, families, or at least the village where they had been born. Whereas Ivan Vostyach had nothing. He was the last survivor of a vanished world. Then I asked myself if we are indeed really salvaging something when we preserve these now vanished languages in formalin like so many freakish animals. Are we not in fact rather pandering to some personal obsession of our own, of no more use to anyone else than a collection of beer mats or cigarette packets? Maybe I'm getting old, but sometimes I feel that all this vainglorious science is beginning to bore me and that one day I shall throw my phonology handbooks out of the window and hurl my tapes of Samoyedic dialects into the stove. But, fight against it as I may, I remain a product of the Soviet Era and I cannot rid myself of the illusion that one day the world will be made comprehensible to us by the power of human reason. You knew me when I was a student, you will remember how passionately we at the institute believed that all things – perhaps even emotions – were susceptible to comparison. Science could explain everything, knowledge was the great panacea. At the time, for us, those strange languages that we collected out in the sticks were diseases, the product of ignorance and barbarism which had to be tracked down and eradicated, so that the pure language of communism could flourish. But the cynical mentality of the scientist is clearly still with me, so I shall bring my Vostyach along to the XXIst Conference on Finno-Ugric languages. Partly in acknowledgement of our longstanding friendship, you are the only person I have told of his existence.

I haven't said anything about my discovery to my colleagues in Saint Petersburg, not even to Juknov, although he's my superior. Dear Jarmo, the times when we shared a scientific passion are long gone – the times when I would write you letters even longer than this to update you on the progress of my research. Perhaps you will be surprised by the sincerity of these pages. You may feel it is misplaced, because we are no longer in such close touch. I know that my discovery will arouse envy and jealousy in the academic world, I know that many of my colleagues will try to put a spanner in the works and dispute its authenticity. I know that you too will find the existence of my Vostyach inconvenient. Nonetheless, I decided to tell my secret to you, and you alone: perhaps because there was a time when everything seemed to me more innocent, when we too spoke a language which has now disappeared: the artless, straightforward language of two students who were full of hope. So, in the name of the enthusiasm we once shared, I am asking you to help me to do all you can to make ensure that Ivan receives a warm welcome in Helsinki and is treated with all possible consideration. We must keep an eye on him, make his time there as pleasant as possible. He must feel that those around him are on his side. I don't want him to feel that he's being treated like an animal at the zoo, or a fairground attraction. After the conference, I've decided to go back to his forests with him and help him to settle back into the village where I found him. All in all, it probably doesn't matter if he carries on living among the Nganasan and forgets his Vostyach. One peaceful human life is surely more important than the survival of the lateral affricative with labiovelar overlay.

Before going back to Saint Petersburg, I had to stop off here in Moscow to get Ivan a passport. It wasn't easy. I had to pull strings and it all took several days. Ivan is completely at sea in a big city. The lighting and the crowds are what bother him most. He hates walking down a busy pavement, and finds the flashing shop signs particularly alarming. By day he stays in his hotel room, and by night I take him walking in the parks. He needs to take long walks in the darkness before he calms down a bit. The plane journey nearly did for him; another flight to Helsinki might really finish him off, so I thought of taking the Friday night train with him which arrives in Helsinki about seven thirty in the morning. But I shall have to stop off at Saint Petersburg because there's a meeting of the academic senate on Saturday night, and after so many months away I can't afford not to be there. So I'm asking you if you'd be good enough to meet Ivan at the station and take care of him for a few hours. I'll be arriving by plane the same evening, on the 19.15 flight. There won't be much for you to do. Leave the hotel booking to me. Your task is just to be with him and make him feel safe. Perhaps you could say something about him to the people at the desk, so that they'll be more understanding. I do hope you can help me. I've talked to Ivan a lot about you. I've told him that you're a dear friend, that you're a scientist, like me, that you study the languages of the men of the tundra and that you wish them well. So he decided he wanted to make you a present – a pipe made from the bone of a falcon, the kind his people play when they go hunting and want to propitiate animal spirits. He'll give it to you when you meet. I'm telling you this because it's important that you show appreciation for this gift. This matters to him – it is a sign of trust.

I'll telephone you on Friday 9th January to make sure that you've received this letter, trusting I'll find you in your office. If I remember rightly, around six o'clock you always used to have a nip of cognac in front of the open window before going down to dinner. And I know you to be a man who doesn't change his habits lightly.

See you soon,
Olga.

Professor Aurtova had just finished reading the last few words when the phone rang.

'Hallo, Olga.'

'Jarmo! Is it still cognac?'

'*Koskenkorva* is for backwoodsmen and vodka is strictly for Russians. All that's left for civilized people is cognac. One day we'll be making an excellent cognac on the banks of the Pyhaharvi.'

'Some people never change, eh?'

'Change implies mistakes.'

'Same old fighting spirit, I see. Is it my Vostyach who's worrying you?'

'It depends how Vostyach he is. He might just be a drunken Kalmuck who got on the wrong train.'

'I see. You didn't like the dig about the red-skins. Come on, I take it all back. Let's bury the hatchet and light the pipe of peace.'

'Don't worry. I'm not on a war footing. Send me your Vostyach by all means. I'm eaten up with curiosity.'

'You'll see, you'll be moved the moment you hear his voice.'

'I'll try not to cry. What time does the train arrive?'

'At 7.48. Ivan will be in coach 16. You can't miss him: he's dressed like a trapper and he always has his drum slung round his neck.'

'I hope he doesn't bite. What does he eat?'

'Very funny. Try roots and berries! But Jarmo, do you really not believe me?'

'I believe you all right. I was just joking. Where will your wild chum be staying?'

'I've booked two rooms at the Torni. I'm not asking you to entertain him. All you have to do is keep him company; above all, don't let him go wandering around on his own. And remember that he doesn't drink alcohol. One more thing: don't talk to him in Russian. That might frighten him. I've assured him that there are no Russians in Finland.'

'What language should I address him in? I warn you, I have no intention of learning Vostyach!'

'I'm sure that if you speak to him in Finnish, but without inflecting the nouns, with the help of the odd gesture he'll understand you. Unless you've still got a smattering of Nganasan.'

'Absolutely not. But I'll manage. Don't worry, I'll take good care of your noble savage. Indeed, for friendship's sake I'll come and meet you at the airport on Saturday evening.'

'Oh, that's sweet of you! It takes a Vostyach to drag a chivalrous gesture out of you!'

'Well, at least he's serving some purpose.'

Aurtova hung up. He downed the last drop of cognac and walked over to the map of the world by Ibn Al-Idrisi, the first geographer to have described the lands inhabited by the Finno-Ugrians in the Middle Ages. He scratched his beard thoughtfully, his attention fixed on the regions occupied by the speakers of Ingrian, Votic, Vogul, Mordvin and Udmurt, each with their different colours, stretching from Karelia as far as the Laptev Sea. At the bottom, in the margin, a dotted blue line indicated the lands supposedly occupied by the mysterious Vostyachs. 'Two thousand wasted years,' he thought. His people had spent two thousand years emerging from the darkness of the steppe. They had struggled, suffered, been in danger of being swept aside by brutal enemies. With admirable persistence they had at last won themselves respect among the European nations, indeed they were gaining a sphere of influence in the lands peopled by their backward linguistic cousins, and Finnish was gradually becoming the *lingua franca* of the Arctic Ocean. But now 'someone' was trying to throw Finland into the dustbin of history, together with the other conquered peoples who have no future. Aurtova was not having that. He looked away from the map and towards the portrait of Marshal Mannerheim, the hero who had twice saved Finland from the Russians. Now it was up to him, Jarmo Aurtova, to save his country. From those same uncouth Vostyachs, no less! The professor clenched his fists. His eyes lit up, and a brief dizzy spell caused him to lose his balance. Suddenly Ibn Al-Idrisi's great map seemed to be positively awash with Finno-Ugrians: speakers of Veps, Ingrian, Nenets and Karagass seemed to be marching over the parchment like so many ants, forming endless black columns which soon scored the entire Siberian plain. The Hungarians were headed directly westwards, leaving speakers of Mordvin and Cheremis behind them. Speakers of Veps, Votic and Permic fanned out along the rim of the Arctic Ocean, while the Sami and Karelians carried on as far as the White Sea. Even the Finnic peoples lingered for a time beside the Pechora before heading firmly southwards towards Lake Ladoga. Samoyeds, Komi and Voguls crossed the Jenisej en masse and spread throughout the upland plains, pushing eastwards in ever-dwindling numbers. Only the Vostyachs never moved away from their Byrranga Mountains. Nervously watching all the others leaving, they wheeled round, clustered together on the shores of the Laptev Sea, and then withdrew into their forests. Peering more closely at the map, the professor saw hunters dressed in skins, hiding behind rocks, bows at the ready. Dark-complexioned, their skin chapped by the wind, they had deep-set narrow eyes and wore necklaces of wolves' teeth around their necks. The women were huddled behind them, their babies wrapped in furs, their sledges, laden with household goods, standing beside reindeer kneeling in the snow. In the distance, a group of yurts had clearly been set on fire and armed horsemen were pillaging the smoking ruins, apparently emitting blood-curdling yells. They must have been Pechenegs or Khazars, who had left the steppe to follow the rivers down to the Arctic Ocean, sacking and slaughtering as they went. Blinking owlishly, Aurtova roused himself from his torpor and suddenly the vision faded, the human anthill disappeared. Now the map was as silent and motionless as it had been before. In his fine wooden frame, Mannerheim was now looking glum. His chest laden with medals, he was gazing into the distance, eastwards, towards the dark Karelian Woods from which the Slavic hordes had once emerged. The sound of his heels ringing out on the gleaming parquet, the professor honoured the marshal's portrait with a military salute, stuffed Olga's letter in his pocket, took his coat from the hatstand and ran down the stairs, forgetting the open windows in his haste, setting the old furniture creaking in the chill night air. A gust of freezing wind sent the curtains billowing and blew the candles out. Outside, it was beginning to snow.

When Margareeta woke up, the first thing she saw in the thin light was the dog. As usual, he was sleeping curled up on one of the small armchairs in her bedroom. He was snoring, his body twitching as he dreamt; his eyelids were fluttering and his front paws quivering. Since Jarmo had left, Hurmo had refused to sleep in the wicker basket under the basin. He would sniff it, whimpering, then pace around it but refuse to go in. It was as though he were afraid that people were leaving the house one by one, abandoning him to his own devices. Each time she looked at him, Margareeta was amazed at how much that dog resembled her husband. It was incredible that a man and a dog could look so alike. Their expressions were similar, they even walked the same way, and when he barked Hurmo would twist his neck in the same irritated fashion that Margareeta had always found so annoying in her husband. She shuddered at the thought that in fact her husband had never left her, but had somehow wormed his way into that snarling ball of matted fur, to carry on tormenting her even after their divorce, just as the Lapp sorcerers befuddled the Lutheran pastors who had been sent to convert them. They would suck their souls from out of their bodies and replace them with evil spirits who drove them mad.

It was now ten days into the new year, and Margareeta was beginning to look forward to a clean break with the past. Hurmo was now all that remained of her husband; he too would have to go, back to his master, together with his fleas. That day would be the last time he would sleep on the little armchair in her bedroom. On waking in the morning, Margareeta no longer wanted to see her husband's canine double snoring at her feet and spreading his stink of ageing fur throughout the house. It was still dark, but Margareeta got up and switched on the coffee percolator. Outside it was snowing. The radio informed her that the recent cold dry snap would be followed by a blizzard. She dressed, gulped down a cup of coffee, put the dog on the lead and dragged him outside. As a matter of fact the dog was a bitch, but no one had been aware of this fact until she had produced five monstrous little mongrels. Or perhaps the creature was both male and female at the same time, somehow fiendishly enjoying the advantages of both sexes. There was no knowing what kind of animal she had coupled with. Like Margareeta's husband, when she was on heat she would go with whatever came to hand: Margareeta thought disgustedly of the big mangy mud-bespattered sheepdog she'd seen sniffing around Hurmo one afternoon in the park. It had been staring vacantly into space as it mounted the bitch, just as her husband probably did when he thrust himself upon his female students, lustful and brutal, bathed in unpleasant male odours.

Frozen and motionless, the city was now emerging from the dawn mist. The odd empty tram rattled along the snow-covered avenues, lights ablaze, bearing gaudy advertisements for tropical holiday destinations. Margareeta felt that she would have to have the dog problem solved before the day was out.

Aurtova walked into the station booking hall breathless and snow-covered. He'd spent a fortune, been punched in the face and had barely four hours sleep, but he had managed to make the necessary arrangements. He felt in his coat pocket to check that the money and envelope with the Silja Line ticket were still there, then ran his fingertips cautiously over his black eye. His steps echoed menacingly in the half-empty booking hall. He glanced at the arrivals board and hurried towards platform 1. The train had clearly arrived some time ago. Cleaners were going up and down it with yellow brooms and rubbish bags. The last passengers were walking towards the exit, pulling on their gloves and turning up their coat collars. He caught sight of someone who looked like one of the hunters he'd seen briefly emerging from Ibn Al-Idrisi's map. Was that the Vostyach? Was that ugly mug the missing link between Finn and Redskin? Between the strong-willed race which had resisted Russian invasion and those primitive headhunters, with their painted faces? Aurtova clenched his teeth until his jaw ached. He would never allow the name of Finnish civilization to be brought into disrepute by some tatterdemalion hominid. Sophisticated Scandinavian design, Europe's most advanced social security system and communications technology could have nothing in common with peoples who had been defeated by history and were now penned into reserves, drinking themselves silly and sporting feather head-dresses in front of slack-jawed tourists. He approached his quarry stealthily, as though fearing it might escape him.

'You Ivan?' he asked quietly, trying to avoid attracting unwelcome attention. The strange figure had a drum slung over one shoulder, and now he drew it closer to his chest.

'Ivan Vostyach!' he shouted, taking his passport from his

pocket and proffering it to Aurtova like a talisman. He gave out a strong smell of wild animal, a circus smell.

'Me Aurtova!' growled the professor, moving backwards a little so as to draw a breathe of a less polluted air. The cleaners were now peering curiously out of the train windows. They had had their eye on the outlandish fur-clad figure pacing the platform for quite some time. Who on earth could he be? A reindeer-breeder? A seal-hunter?

'Aurtova!' Ivan repeated tonelessly, staring at the professor.

'Yes, Aurtova! Friend Olga!' he agreed.

Ivan continued eyeing him from head to foot.

'Friend Olga,' he said flatly.

'Yes, friend Olga!' Aurtova held out his arms and smiled, hoping to appear well-disposed.

Then Ivan felt in his pocket, produced a leather package tied up with a shoelace and handed it unceremoniously to the professor. Aurtova opened it impatiently, to find it contained a curved piece of bone. Then he remembered the business about the pipe. He looked around him in embarrassment. There was no one else on the platform; only the cleaners on the train. They were spending more time than necessary cleaning the last two compartments, darting glances out of the window to see what was going on out on the platform.

'Thanks! Nice work! Fine craftsmanship!' said the professor, turning the object round between his fingers and slipping it into his pocket. But Ivan narrowed his bleary eyes and shook his head. Placing a finger in front of his mouth, he indicated to Aurtova that he should play it. Then the professor remembered what Olga had said about the need for a courteous response. He fished the bone patiently out of his pocket and blew firmly into the little hole. It gave out a piercing whistling sound, like birdsong. The Vostyach smiled and nodded in satisfaction.

'Olga,' he said.

'Olga, yes. Olga say me take you hotel!' said Aurtova, less patient now, stuffing the pipe back into his pocket. He set off towards the exit, indicating to the Vostyach that he should follow him. Ivan picked up his sack and settled his drum more comfortably on his shoulder. They walked through the snow to the underground car park, Aurtova leading and Ivan following, looking around warily and sniffing the air, nostrils aquiver.

He sat down on the seat and placed the drum firmly on his knee, then breathed on the window so as to be able to see out. His gaze was met first by the huge bronze statues on the station façade, holding their lighted torches, then the impressive outline of the Sokos Shopping Centre, standing starkly in the square like a black glass monolith.

'Helsinki,' he said, again flatly, though in fact it turned out to be meant as a question.

'Yes, Helsinki! Suomi, Finland!' was Aurtova's prompt response, as he leant away from his passenger towards the car door in order to avoid contact with his stinking skins. Now the Vostyach was staring open-mouthed at the green dome of the cathedral, with its gilded stars. The professor was looking at Ivan out of the corner of his eye and trying to breathe out through his nose, so as not to have to take in the sickening stench.

'*Suuri, ikivanha heimo!*' exclaimed the Vostyach, pointing towards the buildings. They were the only three words of Finnish that he knew. Olga had taught him them.

'Yes, great and ancient tribe...' repeated an uncomprehending Aurtova.

In the distance, over the sea, there were now glimmers of a hesitant white dawn. But over the city the sky was still dark, tinged greenish-yellow by the lamplight. The headlights of a snowplough came into view along a side street as the vehicle skidded from one side to the other, raising a cloud of dirty snow, which then fell back upon the car, causing Ivan to clutch the seat.

Even though it was early on a Saturday morning, and such few cars as there were, were proceeding with difficulty through the snow, wherever possible Aurtova was taking unfamiliar side roads, hoping to avoid being seen by anyone he knew. In order further to reduce this risk, he had hired a car from the airport. He drew up at the pavement somewhere in Kallio, in front of the unlit window of a run-down bar.

'Hotel,' said the Vostyach.

'Yes, hotel,' the professor agreed. Then he paused for thought. He had been surprised by the Vostyach's tone of voice: when asking a question, after initially rising, it then seemed to fall. Then he remembered the interrogative prefix. Unlike in Finnic languages of the Baltic group, in Proto-Uralic the interrogative particle was thought not to exist. Obviously there must be a tone of voice for expressing a question, but no one had ever been able to distinguish it, and it was impossible to reconstruct it. Perhaps that was what the Vostyach was using. Aurtova was intrigued. For all his current criminal intent, for a moment his mind was once more that of a scientist. Right now – albeit not for very long – he was in the presence of the last Vostyach. He wanted to hear the famous velar affricatives and retroflex palatals with his own ears.

'You speak language of men?' he asked his guest, bringing out Nganasan words at random.

Ivan frowned uncomprehendingly.

'Ivan Vostyach, Vostyach,' he exclaimed in alarm.

'Yes, me understand, Vostyach! Speak Vostyach!' Aurtova urged him, somewhat curtly.

'Speak Vostyach!' Ivan repeated, scarcely more politely.

'*Vostyach, puhukää, sana, wada, may, rääkidi*!' Now Aurtova came out with a volley of Finno-Ugric words.

'Vostyach!' repeated Ivan in exasperation.

Then Aurtova lost patience and turned to Russian:

'In a word, my friend, where are you from? Let's hear a bit about you! Are you really a Vostyach? Or just a dolgan shepherd who wandered into the Tajmyr Peninsula and told Olga a pack of lies? Come on, tell me the truth!'

When he heard his host abandon the friendly sounds of Finnish and move on to the spongy palatalization typical of Russian, Ivan stiffened. Olga Pavlovna had promised him that there were no Russians in Finland. He put the drum on his knee, braced himself with his feet and thrust his back against the door with all his strength, until the window shattered and he was able to wriggle out.

'No, wait, me friend! Jarmo friend of Vostyach! Jarmo little Vostyach!' Aurtova began to plead in Finnish, trying to put on an Estonian accent, which sounded more uncouth. Ivan had run to the corner of a block of buildings and was watching Aurtova's movements with suspicion. The professor had picked up the sack from the back seat and was waving it around slowly, as though it were a bait, as he tried to approach the Vostyach.

'Pardon! I Finnish, no ruski, Suomi, Helsinki! This hotel!' he said quietly, trying not to attract attention. 'Olga this evening arrive here hotel. Olga Vostyach!'

Hearing Olga's name, Ivan calmed down. He turned back towards the car and snatched his sack out of Aurtova's hands.

'Hotel?' the professor suggested in a friendly tone.

'Hotel,' repeated Ivan.

'Good,' answered Aurtova with relief.

They went up the dark staircase of a council house. On the second-floor landing, Aurtova knocked three times and gestured to Ivan to stand back. The door was grudgingly and a threatening face became visible in the semi-darkness.

'The rest of the money!' said the face's owner, putting out a rough, red hand.

Aurtova felt in his pockets. He handed the man a wad of notes held together with an elastic band, and the envelope with the Silja Line ticket.

'The agreement is as follows. You keep him here until this evening, then put him on the 18.15 boat. And remember, make sure he's good and drunk,' hissed the professor through the crack in the door, receiving a grunt by way of answer. The door then closed again, to reopen a few seconds later to reveal a large, thickset man with a flat face peppered with reddish freckles. His nose looked as if the nostrils had been brutally dug out of it with the use of a drill, his eyes were two narrow clefts in the leathery skin. He was wearing a leather jacket which was too small for him, from which his huge hands protruded like lifeless lumps. He looked Ivan over sharply, casting a sneering grimace in the professor' direction. Aurtova took a step backwards, giving the man's gnarled hands a nervous look as they clenched and unclenched. He thought back with disgust to the previous night's humiliation, when he had had to go into that bar to pick up a prostitute in order to be able to speak with the Laplander. Tatiana disgusted him, but she was the only one available. Aurtova had followed her into a room at the back of the bar, though he felt not the slightest desire to lay a finger on that obese reindeer. All he wanted was for her to take him to the Laplander. Aurtova did not know him, indeed he had never even seen him. All he knew about the owner of the 'Unusi Teatteri' was that he was a Laplander and that he had some girls working for him in rooms behind the bar. But Tatiana misread the situation. Thinking that Aurtova was nervous, she pulled out her breasts, pouring champagne over them and laughing. It was only after they had gone into the room, which smelt of unwashed socks, and Aurtova refused to take his clothes off, that the Laplander arrived. Tatiana had pressed a button on the telephone, then put her clothes on again, cursing the while. Seated on the edge of the bed, she was waiting, chain-smoking, swearing furiously the while. The Laplander too was furious, because Tatiana had wasted a whole hour. Then he had punched Aurtova and paid Tatiana as though she were Miss Finland herself. Only afterwards had he heard him out.

They went down the stairs in silence, then into the street and down it to the bar. Day had now broken, but the street-lamps were still alight. A strong wind was raising eddies of snow. The Laplander turned the key and pushed open the bar door.

'Hotel,' said Ivan.

'Yes, hotel,' agreed Aurtova, pushing the Vostyach through the door with a reassuring smile. The place smelt of smoke and stale liquor, and the animal stench that came from Ivan mingled with them, forming a heady brew. In the bruised half-light the wood of the counter and the grimy glass of the windows and mirrors winked back at one another half-heartedly. The soles of their shoes squeaked on the tiles of the beer-drenched floor. Ivan was hanging back, moving forward cautiously into that unknown cave. Aurtova pulled him firmly into the room, as though hoping to cut off his last line of escape. 'Vostyach now rest, this evening Olga! *Hyvää? Hästi*?' he said to him, uttering each syllable with particular care and putting his face threateningly near to Ivan's. The Laplander had opened a door concealed in the wall at the end of the room and was showing Ivan into a lit corridor. Walking backwards between the tables, still covered with dirty glasses and overflowing ashtrays, Aurtova waved goodbye to the Vostyach and went out into the street, then set off hastily towards the car, relieved to be free of his charge but a little disappointed still not to have heard the

52

lateral affricative with labiovelar overlay.

Margareeta didn't even wait for Humro to stop urinating. She dragged him brutally through the snow, where he left a yellow trail. This was the third time she had walked round the block and rung her husband's doorbell, to no avail. Yet his car was parked in front of the house, and Jarmo never went anywhere without his car, not even to the university which was two steps away. Perhaps he had spent the night with one of his cheap prostitutes or was sleeping it off on a friend's sofa. Was it or was it not Saturday morning? Or perhaps he had seen Margareeta from the window and, guessing her intentions, was pretending not to be at home so that he would not have to take the dog. Before the evening was out, either that dog would be reunited with its master, or it would be found the next morning outside the main door, rock-solid as the statue of Haavis Amanda. The weather forecast had proved correct. By the time dawn broke, a bank of cloud was already darkening the sky towards the east. The wind was sending increasingly dense swirls of snow rustling against the window panes. Margareeta decided that it would be wiser to take refuge in some café and eat a nice slice of cake, waiting for the blizzard to die down. She would go back later, hoping to catch Jarmo by surprise; she wouldn't ring the bell, but have herself let in by a neighbour. The Kluuvi Shopping Centre was still empty at that hour. The first shops were rolling up their shutters and the salesgirls were putting on their overalls. A newspaper vendor was hanging up advertisements for the dailies outside his kiosk. Inside the bar, the television was on, but without the sound. Margareeta bought a newspaper and sat down at a table amidst waiters who were still mopping the floor. Hurmo huddled miserably under her chair, his snow-covered fur leaving a little puddle beside him.

The Laplander stopped half-way down the corridor. He opened a door and, after a short delay when Ivan stood obstinately on the threshold, trampling the thick moquette, hustled him in. The room was windowless; a lamp, swathed in scarves, gave out a ruddy light, revealing dark-papered walls, a chest of drawers of varnished wood and a bed with the covers pulled neatly back. The Laplander thrust the Silja Line ticket into the Vostyach's pocket, took a plastic bottle and two glasses out of the fridge, put them on the bedside table and left the room. Ivan looked around him. Two tubular metal light fittings hung from the ceiling, connected to a wire which ran all round it, giving out a dull, unsteady light; they jingled slightly when the Laplander closed the door. The wall at the foot of the bed was entirely covered by a poster depicting a tropical beach. A fish tank containing little coloured fish was gurgling on a console table. Ivan stared at them in delight, and they stared back. A small stick of incense, in a brass brazier shaped like a dragon, gave out a slight thread of smoke. Ivan heard a rustling noise and a sound of running water, coming from behind a curtain. From the other side of the wall came the low cackle of a radio. Somewhere else, a heating pipe was clicking away, giving out a smell of dry paint. Suddenly the curtain twitched, then opened, and a sturdy middle-aged woman appeared, with extremely black hair and a heavily made-up face. She was wearing a black lace leotard, open at the front, revealing red underwear, dangling suspenders and a deep-set belly button in a fleshy fold of skin.

'Hello!' she said, sidling towards Ivan in her little silver clogs in a manner suggestive of some tried and trusted ritual; but then a whiff of rankness, sudden as a slap, brought her up short and forced her to retreat, to collapse abruptly on to the edge of the bed, seized with a fit of coughing, until she could recover herself. Regaining her composure, she adjusted her hair, and leotard. Then she picked up the bottle and filled the two glasses on the bedside table, downing one in a single gulp and reaching out to hand the other to the Vostyach, keeping him prudently at arms' length. Ivan shook his head and backed up against the door. He had never seen a woman dressed like that. He did not know that they wore such items beneath their outer garments. In the turnip-growers' village the innkeeper's wife wore felt boots and voluminous coarse cloth breeches beneath her heavy overcoat. Ivan had seen them once when he was spying on her in the back of the shop. And the eyes of the fair-haired woman who collected his words were nothing like the lying, threatening eyes of the woman he had before him now. He stayed where he was, shaking.

'I'm Katia.' In an effort to stifle an incipient coughing fit the woman now emptied Ivan's glass as well. Swaying her hips, she slipped off her leotard and approached her client, who stared at her in horrified fascination. Making a smacking sound with her fleshy lips, she gave him a slight peck, allowing her breasts to brush against him, but then promptly recoiled, again overwhelmed by the stench.

'And you? What are you called? Where are you from?' She stood with her legs apart, her heels wedged firmly into the carpet. She spoke a broken Finnish, and Ivan could not understand a word of what she said. He stared in bewilderment at the hairless white body he saw wiggling before him.

'Katia,' he repeated in a strangled voice.

'You too?' said the woman, laughing. She took a few steps backwards, put her hands behind her back and undid her bra, which rolled down over her stomach and landed between her feet. Ivan stared at the skimpy red garment where it lay, amazed that something so small could contain so much swollen softness. He would have liked to pick it up and have a closer look. But then his interest was caught by the sight of the woman's chest. Katia took him in her arms and let him spread himself against her, then stretched out on the bed, kicking her clogs into the air. The Vostyach had not so much as loosened a fastening of his heavy leather jacket. Trickles of sweat were making their way down his temples and neck. Now he was shuffling his boots on the moquette, clutching his sack and drum. Bothered by the smoke from the incense, he wrinkled his nose and tried to keep his distance from the brazier; but there was nowhere to retreat to.

'Come on, give them a feel! Just see how smooth they are!' the woman said, stroking her breasts with her hands. Her legs were still apart, and she was moving her pelvis up and down. Under the red triangle of her panties Ivan could now see a black shape from which he found it impossible to look away.

'Come on!' she said again, invitingly. She rolled around on top of the sheets and then lay still, stretched out on her stomach. The Vostyach could still see that mesmerising black shape between her thighs, above those big white buttocks. He felt like touching them. He put his things down and knelt on the bed. First he brushed the white surface with his fingertips, then he felt the soft skin with the flat of his hand. It was warm and tender, he liked pressing it between his fingers, then letting it go and pressing it again, like soft dough which kept the mark of the outline of his hands. She was no ordinary woman, he could see that. She must be a city creature, who had grown up indoors, under electric light, amidst noisy crowds, without ever breathing the cold air of the woods, which flays your skin, makes your eyes stream and hardens your limbs. Such a creature could live only in the stifling heat of this room, she must feed off soap and the white juice in that bottle, and breath the bitter smoke from the little metal mask on the bedside table. Perhaps she had been born of one of the coloured fish in the fish tank. A gleaming little cartilaginous fish, she would have swum in its water and grown up concealed in cold fish scales – yellow and blue and red – which gradually flaked off, revealing her beauty, her seaweed skin. Ivan imagined all the coloured fish in the tank as so many Katias-to-be. Soon they would all be utterly transformed, would emerge from the water in their glorious new incarnation and enfold him in their velvety caresses, in their cool, dripping embrace.

While the Vostyach was exploring her flesh, Katia carried on with her wiggling, emitting false little giggles as she did so. She had lifted her head and was nervously observing Ivan's hands as they explored her body, then finally parted her thighs. She was beginning to lose patience. It was bad enough having to put up with the man's stench. She certainly wasn't going to put on an erotic performance in order to excite him. He'd better undress and get on with it. She tried to slip two fingers into his underpants to get them down, but Ivan pulled them out of her grasp with a blow from one paw-like hand. He then became extremely agitated. His heart was beating violently under the heavy, laced up skins. Hot beads of sweat were falling from his eyebrows into his eyes, his ears were burning, his legs were trembling, the veins in his temples, taut as bowstrings, throbbed to the rhythm of his breath. He leant forward over the black shape, which had now become one with the shadow of the sheet, and pressed his whole hand down on it. It felt warm, damp and sticky, like the torn belly of a hare when you put in a hand to pull out the innards. He touched flesh as tender and smooth as entrails. He was expecting to smell their bitter stench, the sweetish aroma of blood. But his nostrils met with a different smell entirely, one which took his breath away and caused his eyes to mist over, leaving him unable to move. The woman turned over on her back and pulled him up on to the pillow beside her. She began to touch his lips and caress his forehead, sinking her fingers into his hair. Ivan half-closed his eyes. No one had ever caressed him before, no hand ever been placed so gently on his forehead. Katia slipped her fingers slowly into the neck of his jacket. She was breathing through her mouth, trying to undo the leather knots so that she could ease him out of those foul skins. But Ivan was on his guard, and when he felt her pulling on the knots he pushed her hand away. The scent of that skin, which smelt of sugar, the sight of that spotless body beneath his own, made his head swim, as it did when he had spent a sleepless night drumming for his wolves to come to him. A melting feeling stole over him, a swooning sense of sweet abandonment. Still dressed from head to foot in his putrid skins, his feet still in his sodden boots, he threw himself upon the woman, clasping her to him, clutching her as though he wanted to claw the flesh from her every limb, tear her to shreds and stuff the pieces into his mouth. Katia tried to calm him, to regain the initiative, but Ivan was now seized with a fury there was no assuaging. He unlaced what had to be unlaced and thrust himself brutally between her thighs with a hoarse moan. A scream sent the fish scurrying off to a corner of the tank. Ivan tensed his muscles and slammed her down on to the bed, tightening his grip, rejoicing in his exploration of every last nook and cranny of that white body, digging his nails into the yielding flesh, watching her veins swell and her breasts quake. His body was burning, drops of his sweat were falling on to Katia's chest in greasy globules. But he could not stop himself: he clung to her grimly, crushing her beneath him, breathing in her sweetish smell, mingled with the stench of animal fat and mud from his own rough skins. Suddenly the bed collapsed on to the bedside table, knocking off the lamp, which did not shatter, but rolled off in the direction of the fish-tank. There on the ground, in the tangle of sheets, he felt a spasm shoot through his whole body, biting as a whiplash; his stomach contracted with a stab of pain. Then his limbs seemed to melt, the blood to flow more smoothly in his veins. He loosened his grip. He lifted his sweat-drenched head and opened his mouth, gasping for air in that incense-laden room. Beneath him, Katia was no longer laughing, or swaying her hips. She was staring fixedly at the metal light fittings hanging from the ceiling. Across her neck ran a red trickle, though in the dim lighting it looked black. It started from behind her ear, then spread over the now matted hair on the nape of her neck. Horrified, Ivan looked at his hands. Muffled sounds were now coming from somewhere beyond the wall, becoming more distinct, moving in his direction. Someone was rattling at the door, causing it to bang against the bedstead. An angry voice was shouting threatening words in Russian. Ivan clenched his fists, and braced himself. In his mind's eye, he saw the chinks of light between the boards of the hut, smelt the smell of burnt urine, heard the steps of the soldiers on the snow, the sound of gunshots in the darkness. The door burst open with a splintering sound and the Laplander hurtled into the room, causing the bed-head to knock into the fish tank. A spurt of red water gushed from the fragments of glass and the coloured fish slithered away, over the grubby carpet, over Katia's breasts and legs. They darted around, then settled on the black shape that had caused Ivan such consternation. In contact with the water, the lamp sputtered, gave out blue sparks and exploded, plunging the room into total darkness.

'Now look what you've done, you animal!' shrieked the Laplander, beside himself as he lunged around the room, trying to locate the Vostyach in the pitch-darkness and pushing pointlessly against the bed, which was now jammed between the wall and the bedside table. Fumbling around on the floor in the sodden chaos, Ivan picked up his sack and his drum. He sat there, squatting in the shadows, muscles tensed, then flung himself upon the figure he could dimly see coming towards him, knocking it to the ground so that he could make his getaway. He slipped into the corridor, crossed the empty bar-room, heaved the street door open and ran off into the snow.

II

'The Ice Age is back: the Gulf of Finland freezes over for the first time in fifty years,' shrieked the headlines. Margareeta leafed through the first few pages of the paper, her mind elsewhere. Reading was the last thing she felt like doing. She pushed aside her coffee cup and asked the waiter for a sheet of paper.

Dear Jarmo,

I'm sitting in a dismal bar, drinking a cup of coffee before bringing Hurmo back to you, and I don't know why I'm writing you this letter. Perhaps because my desire to insult you is so strong that I can't contain myself, I can't wait until I see you face to face. Or perhaps because, by writing, I cherish the fond hope that I shall find the perfect words to rid my mind of you for ever. It's incredible how something new always comes up, even though I think I've said all that's to be said, and everything has been done to death by repetition. It's true, words between the two of us are meaningless. You've killed them stone-dead with your falsehoods, with fifteen years of indifference, silence, betrayal. You've saved whole languages from extinction, but caused the one we spoke between ourselves to die. Now all I want to do is harm you, and my only regret is that I shall never manage to do as much hurt to you as you've done to me. It's too late, you got away before I could land my punches. What's left of you for me is Hurmo. I could take it out on him. I'm not ashamed to tell you that sometimes I've thought of lashing out at him, with you in mind. Perhaps I would have felt a certain satisfaction from hearing him squeal, seeing your face in his panic-stricken snout. I found myself wondering what sort of look would come on to your face if I suddenly started kicking you. Amazement? Outrage? Fear? I'd be willing to pay someone good money to find out. Those are the depths to which I've sunk! No court could ever compensate me for such humiliation. But today I'm bringing Hurmo back to you, returning the last hostage of our life together. I realized too late that you only married me because you needed someone to link arms with at faculty cocktail parties, because only couples would be invited to attend the burgomaster's ball. Unwittingly, like everyone else around you, I too served your ambitions; the only people you've ever wanted to have around you are those who can be of use to you in some way. The same goes for your masters. If you began to be unfaithful, it was because that too served your purposes. Your heart wasn't really in your philandering: new entanglements just meant one more birthday, one more phone number, one more make of perfume and a bunch of flowers to be remembered. When I first discovered that you had a lover, I was surprised: you'd chosen a woman who greatly resembled me. Leena Isotalo might have been my double – an uglier version, if you don't mind my saying so. Idiot that I was, perhaps that was why I forgave you. Unconsciously, I tried to tell myself that you just couldn't get enough of me, that you had to surround yourself with women who were like me. They were just poor copies, idols serving to glorify me without diminishing your adoration. I was the Virgin, they were the statues. Such are the contortions the mind is capable of when it wishes to blind itself to the truth! I now see that you chose lovers who looked like me purely for practical reasons: because black underwear suits all blondes, and one more fair hair on your jacket would escape my notice. I never had the guts to check on it, but I bet they didn't live far from us. That way you could pay them a quick visit of an evening with the excuse of taking Hurmo for a walk. You were never one to do more than the strictly necessary, you weren't one to put yourself out. There's not a moment of your time that isn't put to good purpose. By the time you die, you'll have squeezed every drop out of life. It will spit you out in disgust, it will be sick of you, will shuffle you off like some revolting worm. I, on the other hand, devoted fifteen years of my life to you. My only regret is that there is nothing to show for it. My women friends say we should have had a child. Perhaps it's true. Perhaps a son would have made you less self-centred. Or would he just have been one more person to compete against? At least I wouldn't be alone, I wouldn't be getting up at dawn like a lost soul, wondering how to spend my empty day. Whereas the only living thing to have come out of those fifteen years is this wretched dog, a gift from your friend Pekka, architect and faggot. That must be why he passed it off as male, when in fact it was a bitch. But in your mind even Hurmo was to serve a purpose. He was to add to the picture of the modern young couple with a four-wheel drive and a bouncy, tail-wagging dog. Perhaps it was he who brought us bad luck. Today I'm returning him to you. He is our marriage: ugly, besmirched and past his prime.

Margareeta.

Margareeta left the letter inside the newspaper, counted out the change for the coffee and marched off, dragging Hurmo unceremoniously by the lead. The waiter picked up the cup and wiped under the chair, removing the puddle the dog had made. Before throwing the paper into the waste-paper bin, he cast an inattentive eye over the headlines.

Outside, the city was coming to life. Despite the snow, in the town centre the avenues were full of cars, making their way slowly forwards with their headlights on. Nothing was going to come between them and their Saturday shopping spree, and the shopping centres were filling up, windows ablaze, the whole snow-covered city was abuzz. Christmas had come and gone, but the apartment blocks in the centre were once more glittering with festive lights. Today was a special day. Nature had firmly reasserted herself, and for once could not be kept at bay by central heating systems, neon signs, the smoke from factory chimneys and the mighty ice-breakers moored alongside the quays, awaiting orders to rid the sea-lanes of ice. In the port, sirens were breaking a fifty-year silence, and the weather centre was giving hourly reports on the advance of the ice floes in the gulf. Murmansk, Saint Petersburg, Petrozavodsk and Vaalimo were registering polar temperatures. Radio messages were continually arriving from Tallinn. On the other side of the gulf you could walk on the sea and reach the island of Prangli by car. On such a day, a thousand years ago, hordes of wild men had arrived by sea to sack the Finnish villages, burn down the houses, ravish the women and carry off the children. In defiance of that distant memory, the whole city was now on the alert. It was making as much noise as it possibly could, putting on all its lights, turning the heating systems up to maximum, making a show of all its wealth and strength, as though in a bid to fend off the wild hordes of yesteryear. Let them try attacking Finland now!

Margareeta tried calling Jarmo from every phone box she came upon, to see whether he'd returned home so that she could pay a surprise visit. But all she succeeded in doing was spending her change for nothing, because the phone in the flat in Liisankatuno was never answered by anyone except the answer-phone. She even went back to ring the bell, invented an excuse to have the main door opened by a neighbour and walked up to his landing to shout and bang at his door until the other occupants forcibly expressed their disapproval. She had then waited in the street, keeping a close eye on his windows. But the snow fell silently on windowsills and balconies without any sign of life becoming visible behind the curtains. Yet Margareeta was sure that her ex-husband was at home, probably enjoying the company of some little whore he'd picked up the previous evening. Walking around Liisankatu, she found that she was talking to herself, railing against the dog. The few passers-by shuffling along the icy pavements looked at her as though she were a madwoman, or a drunk. When the cold became unbearable, and the whole street turned into a pit of whirling snow, Margareeta, now exhausted and frozen to the marrow, resigned herself to going home. But she had lost nothing of her determination and, all in all, felt somewhat reassured. She knew where she would certainly be able to find him later. On Saturday evenings Jarmo would unfailingly pay a visit to the Café Engel before dinner. Just to get himself noticed, shake a few hands, arrange a meeting, offer an aperitif to an attractive woman, or indeed to anyone who might be of use to him. All in all, Margareeta thought, there was no hurry. Indeed, it might be even more amusing to hand the dog over in a public place, to embarrass Jarmo in front of his friends, maybe even spoil his evening.

On entering her flat she was met by a stale bedroom smell, mingled with that of cold coffee and the muddy stench of Hurmo. The flat looked charmless and messy in the half-light, and Margareeta felt a wave of sadness. The place smelt like an old peoples' home. She went to throw open the windows, heedless of the snow which blew in and melted on the floor, the furniture, the old wedding photos she hadn't had the heart to throw away. She waited until the room was truly freezing before closing them again. Then she retreated into the bathroom to have a good cry. She undressed, letting her clothes fall in a heap in a corner. She turned on the taps and crouched beside the bath, waiting for it to fill. She watched her white body pucker and then vanish into the mirror as it misted over, as she had done when she was a child. Then, suddenly, she sensed it was too late: to extract her revenge, to mourn, to start afresh, find happiness again. Her life was over, there would be no new beginnings: it had been a catalogue of words and gestures she no longer had the courage to repeat. Behind the door, Hurmo was pressing his nose against the chink of light, pointlessly expectant, scratching at the parquet and whimpering in the darkness, as though he too was eager to make his escape from that ghost-infested flat. When Margareeta emerged from the bath, locks of damp hair were falling over her tear-stained eyes; she was no longer crying, and although her lips were trembling, her jaw was set. She stood barefoot in front of the fridge and had a bite to eat, tossing a scrap to Hurmo as she did so. Then she drank a cup of cold coffee and went back to bed. She set the alarm for five, put in her ear-plugs and pulled the covers over her head. Hurmo had the good sense to wait until his mistress was asleep before returning to his little armchair in the bedroom.

While he was dressing Katia's corpse, the Laplander cursed the day he had left the woods of Airisselka and gone to seek his fortune in the big city. He had left because he had had enough of being drenched to the marrow ferrying tree trunks down the Miekojärvi and sleeping in the open air like an animal. He had had enough of scratching a living by working for those bandits at the sawmill at Pessalompolo. He too wanted to live in a modern flat, to drink Australian wine and womanize to his heart's content, like the lorry drivers who came to load up the timber and would give him bottles of foreign liquor and pornographic magazines. This was what had decided him to move to Helsinki. He had spent his entire savings on the purchase of a bar in a dismal working-class area; but his outgoings were considerable, and his earnings meagre. The licence to sell alcoholic drinks alone cost an arm and a leg. Things didn't look up much even after he had installed various video games. Then he had had that bright idea of smuggling a couple of prostitutes over the border from Saint Petersburg, and two soon became four. At first he had them working in turns in the one-room flat he rented above the bar. Then he decided to close down the gaming room and turn it into four smaller rooms, and it was these that were now his most profitable line of business. He had made a name for himself: the Laplander, they called him. Things had improved, admittedly, but at a price: clients who failed to pay and had to be roughed up, squabbles among the girls for the best room, drug addicts arranging to meet on his premises and locking themselves in the toilets to do business, and the ever-present fear of the police. Four years into that life, there was still no sign of the modern flat of his dreams, he was still drinking shoddy Finnish beer rather than Australian wine, and the only women he could afford to hire were those four wrecks. At times, he even thought back to his tree trunks with something approaching nostalgia. At least they couldn't speak; they never complained, the most resistance they put up was when they ran aground in the mud, and even then they could be easily dislodged. All in all, he thought, life was much easier in a wooden hut on the banks of a lake than on the fourth floor of a dismal council block, and the dainty little creatures in his pornographic magazines were much more biddable than the four rowdy Caucasian trouble-makers he'd so unwisely imported into his living quarters.

Seated on the pink sheets, legs a-straddle, completely dressed apart from her shoes, Katia looked like a wax doll. It was a shame that her head, beneath the jauntily-positioned fake fur cap, persisted in drooping in a way that was undoubtedly somewhat sinister. Clad in their fishnet tights, her legs, too, had lost their beauty; they were now so much inert flesh, and the effect was monstrous. The Laplander had put the red room carefully to rights. He had picked up the dead fish, the broken lamp, the bottle of *koskenkorva*, the torn-off lock and the bits of glass and put the lot into a rubbish bag, together with Katia's wet underwear and the bed linen. He'd straightened out the bedside table, remade the bed with fresh linen and done what he could to mend the door. The water, and Katia's blood, had left a dark stain on the carpet. Luckily, at that hour the bar was closed. At least he had had the idea of sending the other three to ply their trade in a hotel room for that one night. He'd make less out of it himself, of course, but he calculated that the business with the wild man would amply compensate for that. Who could ever have dreamt that he'd end up killing her? And of course it would have to be Katia, the best of the lot, the one who could bring in as much as fifty marks a night! It was the first time anyone had died on him, though he'd heard that this could happen. The best thing would be to dump her body in a stolen car with a syringe stuck in her arm. But the others would take fright when they heard what had happened. They might even run away, and the Laplander couldn't afford to lose the lot of them in one fell swoop. Another solution was called for. Seated on the bed beside the dead woman, the erstwhile lumberjack from Airisselka put on his thinking cap. It was only ten in the morning, but some bright idea had to hit him pretty fast.

Aurtova hung up and eased his neck backwards with a sigh. Another thing achieved: now he had managed to book a double room in the Torni under the name of Boris Juknov. He put his gloves on again and wiped a hand over the misty glass of the phone box to check that no policeman had removed his car from the no-parking area where he'd left it. He looked at the clock on the television tower. He had plenty of time, but he would have to proceed with care. Now the second half of his plan would come into play. The first thing to do was to call in at his flat. Here he collected two bathrobes, two silver candlesticks, a box of scented candles, an elegant suit (but not the one he would wear at the conference), a pair of silk pyjamas, sheets and blankets; perhaps more importantly, he also remembered the little bottle of green tablets he kept in the medicine cupboard. He had to stifle a shudder as he picked up a packet of contraceptives. Then he went into the garage to patch up the car window as best he could, stuffing a plastic covered sleeping bag into the gap. Into the boot he put a jerrycan of petrol, some anti-freeze spray for locks, a shovel, three bottles of champagne, a compass, a gas cylinder, matches, a torch, some jute sacks, an axe and the snow chains. He took a rope and a clasp knife out of the box of fishing-tackle. Just to be on the safe side, he did his shopping out of town, in the shopping centre at Itäkeskus. There he purchased smoked salmon, some ready-made *piirakka*, reindeer pâté, a packet of savoury biscuits, a frozen wood grouse, some butter, a jar of gherkins, a bag of ready-cooked potatoes, a tub of lemon sorbet, four bottles of Bulgarian cabernet and one of Polish vodka. By midday he was ready to leave. He went down to the tourist harbour and stopped on the Merisatama Quay to fit the snow chains. Other cars were venturing along the track that linked Helsinki to the islands of the archipelago by way of a sea that had frozen over for the first time in half a century. Voices and shadows passed nearby, then were engulfed once more by the soft, clean-smelling silence. There had been a heavy snowfall, and now a chill wind was blowing down from the woods, locking the world under a hard glassy breast-plate. The red pickets were scarcely visible above the sweep of sea, but the bed of the track was sound, made level by the passing of a recent snowplough. Along the shore Aurtova could still see the lights of the occasional vehicle headed for Suomenlinna, briefly glimpsed the lights of Harakka, then nothing. Now the white wall was opening up a metre at a time before the yellow beam of the headlights. It was a good half-hour before the island of Vasikkasaari came into view. Approaching the quay, he turned the lights off, left the main track and reached the waterline. He wanted to get to his cottage avoiding the main road. In all probability, the weather being what it was, there was no one on the island, and both the Kuusinen and the Lehtinen were tucked safely away in their cosy flats in Helsinki. But you could never be too careful. On the north shoreline the wind had swept the snow away. The sea was a bare crust; under the trees it had hardened into mounds.

Villa Suvetar soon came into view. He left the car behind the hedge which served as a windbreak and carried his load into the lumber room. The first thing he did was to remove the protective covering from the generator and link it up with the mains. In winter there was no one in the cottage, and the electricity was turned off, so a petrol generator had to be used to produce electricity. He cleaned the spark-plugs, filled the tank to the brim and cranked up the starting handle. The filaments of the bulb on the wall began to glow, then the light came on in the lumber room. Aurtova picked up the shovel and freed the cottage entrance of ice, just enough so as to be able to open the door. He sprayed the padlocks with the anti-freeze and went into the house. There was plenty of dry wood already on the veranda, but Aurtova went to get some more from the lumber room anyway: the sauna stove was going to have a long night of it. He lit the fire, took the provisions into the larder, fitted the gas cylinder to the stove, spread the biscuits with the reindeer pâté, uncorked the cabernet, laid the table for two and put the candlesticks in place. He made up the bed in the spare room, but also the double bed, laying his silk pyjamas on the left-hand pillow. Then he went to hang up the bathrobes near the sauna door, hung one of his suits in the cupboard in the entrance and put on the other, the smarter of the two. Then he took off his shoes and threw himself down on the divan, to catch a few hours sleep. But he was awoken by dreams of ferocious Pecheneg horsemen, encamped some distance away, around huge bonfires. They were massacring the prisoners they had taken in Finnish villages, tearing limbs from still living bodies and roasting them on the flames, their shrieks audible amidst drum rolls and cruel laughter. Their horses were grazing peacefully some way off, unmoved by all that horror, dragging their hooves insistently over the ground in search of edible roots.

At last, beyond the deafening pit across which yellow and red lights darted in merciless succession, he could see darkness. He had been wandering around the city for hours, trying to find some way out. He had crossed the railway and fetched up in an unending stream of stationary cars, surrounded by great lit-up signs which came and went, one colour vanishing to be replaced by a dozen others. He had been pursued by threatening men who had shrieked at him and lobbed bottles and debris in his direction. But the worst thing was that light, all around him, those dazzling, intrusive headlights. Ivan grasped the wire fencing and sniffed the air. Between the whiffs of diesel he could smell seaweed, and mud. He threw the sack over the fencing, but not the drum. He bound it tightly to his waist. Then he climbed up and jumped down the other side. Dozens of lorries, like those at the mine, were roaring over the asphalt, sending the snow skittering off towards the roadside, where it piled up and immediately hardened under the lashing wind. Ivan shook himself down, tensed his muscles and sprinted off. Lorries hooted their horns, wet tyres skidded over the slippery asphalt, cars came to a gentle halt beside the piles of snow. Then the traffic would set off again in a more orderly fashion, the horns would fall silent and the roar of the engines start up again as before. Ivan had thrown himself down, stomach first, into the blue snow. Now he made off towards the open spaces, turning round every so often to look nervously in the direction of the ruddy embers of the lights as they frizzled in the driving snow. Before long, he found himself facing the silent, open sea, a violet light throbbing overhead. A sudden breath of wind would send the snow whirling up into the air, then settling down again like glass on the petrified surface of the waves. Just as it had done on the waters of the frozen lake where his father had taken him fishing as a child. When they went home, the darkness would follow them as far as the first birches on the beach. It would roll silently among the trees, white totem poles against a pitch-dark sky, while in the distance the ice would close up again with an alarming snapping sound. The string of fish they'd caught would glitter as they made their way along the path, silvery scales catching the dying light. Then all that was left was the dull reflection of the snow. Once they were over the hill, though, they would see the glare of the fire. Inside the yurt, all faces would glow red, so many carvings gashed with long black furrows, like the masks hanging from the ceiling. Ivan remembered how he would test the temperature by collecting a ball of saliva in his mouth, spitting it up into the air and hearing a slight thud as it fell to earth. That meant the coots would not be flying; the fire no longer had the air it needed to burn, and animal droppings would give out no smell.

Ivan was walking cautiously, breaking the crust of the snow with his heels so as not to slip. He did not know where he was going, but some deep instinct seemed to be guiding him. A strip of blackness was approaching from among the clouds which were flying off towards the open sea, making a sound like timber shattering. Soon he found himself among the marble trunks of a birch wood. Above him, the branches cracked like whips at every gust of wind; then they would wave around without touching one another, crackling in the air as though they were about to catch fire. Ivan came to a stretch of coast lit up by faint lights which trembled against the sky. Trapped in the ice, a landing-stage ran from the water's edge, only to disappear into the snow-covered dunes. Inside the wood, beyond the black posts of an enclosure, he could hear something moving. He bent down, sniffed the air and moved into the lee of the wind, to find that the posts had wire netting attached to them. He went around it, without touching it, until he came to the trunk of a big broken pine. He climbed up it, sat down on the thickest branch and observed the landscape below him. It had stopped snowing, but the wind was now blowing harder, dislodging lumps of snow from the pine branches. The thuds they made as they landed sounded like the footsteps of some huge, mysterious creature crashing around in the dark wood. To the west, the cowl of smoke obscuring the sky was lifting, revealing gritty-looking clouds. Then suddenly a red gash rent the horizon, sending out a glancing light which broke against the trunks of the birches. In the enclosure, the wolves' eyes glinted briefly in the sunlight. Then the snow was once more engulfed in sooty shadow, and the wood sank back into darkness. It had all happened very quickly, but Ivan had had time to glimpse the white breath thickening beneath his tree, to hear the wolves whining, then curling up below him. He put his drum on his knee, picked up the bone drumstick and began to play. Quietly at first, brushing the bone against the still cold skin, bound tightly to the fir-wood frame. Then more loudly, allowing his whole body to be taken over by the powerful rhythm which seemed to issue from the earth itself, locked beneath its crust of snow. The animals in Korkeasaari Zoo had never heard the men of the tundra playing the drum. They had been born behind bars, had fed on lumps of frozen meat tossed into their enclosures by the zookeepers; yet that compelling, full-throated beat drew them all from their lairs. They peered around them, nostrils aquiver to catch the scent of the being who was calling them. Then the bear turned in its sleep and let out a roar, the wolves began to howl, scratching at the bark of the viburnum bushes, the reindeer cantered nervously around their pen, sending their manger flying; there on their perches, the arctic falcons spread their wings, the lynxes gnashed their teeth and dug their claws into the stakes of the fencing and the owls, their feathers ruffled with alarm, peered with blind eyes into the gathering darkness.

Hearing life rustling around him, Ivan played more and more loudly. He was sweating now, his whole body was shaking and he heard a deep sound of song welling up from within his body, becoming louder still as it floated clear of the trees. Still as statues, the animals listened to its ancient words. They were in awe of the being which knew all their names, whose drum could mimic the mysterious beat which came from the depths of the earth. After a time, his arms aching unbearably, drunk with exhaustion, his head swimming, Ivan climbed down from his tree and stretched out in the snow. The only sound now was the wind as it soughed through the wood. Then, in the gathering darkness, Ivan saw the child again. It was a long time since he had paid him a visit. How had he managed to follow him all that way? Ivan would have liked to ask him. But he knew that spirits cannot speak. You have to look at them for a long time in silence in order to understand what they have to say. Ivan thought of his distant forest, of the stony track above the mountain stream, of his own people, imprisoned in another world. He should never have abandoned them. They needed him. Olga had promised him that she would take him home. But where was Olga? Why had she left him in that evil city? And where was that great and ancient tribe which was his own? Ivan felt that the path leading up from the woods, beyond the lake, into the tundra, was lost to him forever; as were the stumpy shapes of the Byrranga Mountains, which reminded him of a deer's head, and those two pointed rocks like a hare's ears. That land where, for a little time, he had been happy, where the shade of his father was always at his side, taking the form of a tree or a silent bear, whose voice spoke straight to his own heart. New gusts of stronger wind were now blowing in from the open sea; it was one vast wilderness, but on occasions the glassy crests of the waves would give out a liquid light. The child had disappeared. Now Ivan knew what he had come to tell him. He must go back: before it was too late, before the voice of his people vanished forever and became one with the howling of the wolves.

Squatting against the trunk of the pine, Ivan waited till total darkness fell. Perhaps he slept, perhaps he had fainted from exhaustion. He was awakened by the sound of icy fragments being swept along the ground. The blizzard had died down. The north wind had driven away the clouds and now the air was clear. In the distance, beyond the dark strip of sea, the city lights were causing the shadows to dissolve into a mass of green. Out in the open sea, the solid ice would catch the light and glint like quartz, then be swallowed up in even greater darkness. An abyss of fragile stars had opened up across in the sky, and it was as though the icy breath which was keeping everything motionless came straight from them. Ivan followed the fencing round the enclosure and found himself by some hothouses. He rubbed at the glass, hoping to see inside, but it was pitch black. Further on was a restaurant. Blue lights on the walls lit up the chairs which had been piled on to the tables, and on the pile of sunshades and deckchairs heaped up against the veranda. Ivan followed the row of street lamps and saw a lighted window in the distance.

One hand in a packet of potato crisps, the watchman was sitting in an armchair and drinking a can of beer, waiting for the hockey match to start on television. He had taken off his shoes and was stretching out his feet in front of the stove, enjoying the sensation of rubbing one big toe against the other. Ivan crept past the window, avoiding the lamplight that fell around the entrance to the watchman's lodge, and vanished into the shadow of a block of low buildings. He opened a door at random and found himself in a tool-shed. He selected an axe, a knife and some rope, put them into his sack and, on leaving the shed, also picked up the pair of cross-country skis which the watchman had put for safe keeping behind the door. Thus equipped, he went back to the enclosures, each of whose entrances was lit by a small lamp. The first he freed were the wolves. On hearing someone approach the netting, they all began to howl. But when they heard the bolt being drawn, they stopped howling and rushed towards the gate, stopping short in front of Ivan in some alarm, sniffing the air cautiously, as though they feared a trap. Lowering their ears, they trooped out almost furtively. They didn't move off straight away, but paused for a moment to observe the Vostyach warily, snarling as they did so. Then their white breath disappeared into the darkness. The wild llamas moved in a pack, one serving as a look out for them all. They did not discover that the gate was open until Ivan had reached the enclosure with the pandas. Then they ran out, stretching their necks in glee, ambling past the watchman's lodge and hesitating in puzzlement before galloping off into the open. When Ivan broke the glass of their neon-lit monkey-house, the baboons started to chatter in unison, then rushed en masse to the top of the mangy tree growing in the centre of the enclosure. The little ones took advantage of the situation to leap on to the tractor tyre which hung from the tree on a chain, and stayed there, swinging to and fro, heedless of their mothers' impatient cries as they came down to haul their infants unceremoniously upwards. Ivan watched in delight as those tiny, hairy, man-like creatures clung to the branches, sticking out their tongues at him and gesticulating, uttering uncouth squeals as they did so. His entrance into their warm, evil-smelling cage was met with a shower of excrement and rind. Ivan beat a hasty retreat and went to open the next gate. He had never seen black and white striped horses before. With a wave of his arm, he gestured to them to leave their pen, but they slithered hopelessly over the icy ground, lashing out randomly with their hooves and breathing nervously through quivering nostrils. The lynxes on the other hand shot out in a flash, following the arctic foxes and the chamois, which had sniffed danger in the nick of time. The Siberian tiger let out a fearful roar as it leapt down from the artificial rock into which its cave was set. Then it stood there motionless, jaws agape, staring at the expanse of sea before slipping silently into the darkness. The walrus, the mountain goats, the rabbits, the owls and the wolverines did not notice that their cage doors were open, some because they were in a state of hibernation, others because they had no idea that they could simply walk away. But, on what was recorded as the coldest night in Helsinki for fifty years, all the creatures in Helsinki Zoo had the opportunity of a lifetime.

Ivan stopped in front of the reindeer pen. He selected two young birch trunks and felled them with his axe. Measuring out two identical lengths of wood, he made them into runners, laid them on the ground and fixed them to the watchman's skis. Then he cut six shorter crosspieces and tied them to the runners, to form a sledge. He fashioned a curved branch into an approximation of a yoke and attached it to the two ends of the runners. Then he opened the gate, selected the two strongest reindeer and yoked them to the sledge. He loaded his possessions on to it, picked up a long thin branch, made it into a whip and cracked it expertly over the backs of his reindeer-team. Slithering over the virgin snow, which parted with a hiss beneath his skis, the Vostyach drove out of the zoo towards the open sea, the better to see the stars.

Aurtova and the Laplander left at the same time: Aurtova from Vantaa airport, with a live woman seated in the back, the Laplander from a dismal street in Kallio, with a dead one, her body held in place by a rear-seat safety belt. Their paths crossed, though they did not know it, on the bridge at Kulosaari. How could they have recognized each other, amidst the frenzied traffic plunging into that dark sea?

'It's very good of you to meet me,' said Olga, leaning her elbows on the seat in front of her, trying to catch Aurtova's eye in the rear-view mirror. The front seat was still partly occupied by the sleeping bag in the plastic sheeting, so he had asked her to sit in the back. The professor leaned his head back a little to avoid her gaze, wrinkling his nose in ill-disguised disgust. That woman had always irritated him: by her ugliness, first and foremost. Aurtova found ugliness alarming, particularly in women. He was afraid it might be catching, like bad luck. Secondly, he loathed her total honesty in matters scientific, the implacable conscientiousness with which she went about her work and her modest way of proving herself right, made even more unbearable by the fact that she never wallowed in her triumphs. He thought back to the Russian student he'd known at the university when he himself was still a student in his final year. Kalle Holmberg, the Professor of Uralic Philology, had introduced her to him with much pomp and circumstance, asking him to take her under his wing during the academic year she was to spend in Helsinki. That shy, tubby girl had stuck to him like a shadow, failing to realize that his interest in her was in no way personal, but merely a result of his self-serving desire to do as Holmberg had asked. Her maddening self-effacement, combined with her very considerable grounding in every branch of linguistics, only compounded his dislike. For months on end Aurtova had had to endure the company of this pedantic swot, feign interest in her writing and endlessly discuss dry-as-dust matters of philology. It was only to please Holmberg that Aurtova in his turn had agreed to spend a term at the university of Leningrad, working on a thesis on homo-organic fricatives in the Permic languages. If there was to be any hope of obtaining that longed-for post as a research assistant, the old luminary would have to be soft-soaped. So in Leningrad too he had had to put up with the company of a woman who was as devoted to science as a nun to her vocation. Aurtova was certain that his high-principled Russian colleague would milk her finding of the Vostyach for all it was worth, demolishing the theory of the evolution of the Finno-Ugric languages he'd built up so laboriously over years of study as she did so. She had to be stopped before it was too late. Aurtova had already devised a possible trap but, in order for it to work, he had to remain on good terms with his guest: he had to amuse her, distract her, gaze into her eyes as he talked to her; act in such a way that she felt completely at her ease, suspecting nothing; if absolutely necessary, even seduce her. He braced himself and glanced furtively at his watch: it was a quarter to eight. The Vostyach would be far away by now, somewhere in the Baltic Sea, on his way to Stockholm.

'Duty, dear Olga. We are in Finland, are we not? So it's me who plays the host, just as I did twenty years ago,' he answered affably.

'Well, you haven't always been so welcoming,' she observed sharply, immediately regretting what she'd said. She wiped the car window and stared vaguely out at the lights of the snow-covered city.

'Where have you left Ivan? In the hotel?' she asked after a brief silence, her voice betraying a certain apprehension. Aurtova had read the question in her eyes when she had come up to him in the airport lounge. Her expression had darkened visibly when she saw that the Vostyach was not there. She had offered her cheek to her colleague for a welcoming peck, but her eyes were seeking out the stocky little figure of her prize discovery.

'I went to meet him, as I said I would, so he could come with me to the airport. But he was exhausted, not to mention thoroughly bewildered. He asked for something to eat, then lay down on his bed, fully dressed, and immediately fell asleep. The journey and all those new places must have worn him out. Then today, so as not to have him cooped up in the hotel all day, I took him out of town. Before the blizzard started we went to look at the sea at Kesäranta, and then to Töölonlahti to watch the skaters.'

'In Moscow too he used to get up at dawn and go to bed at dusk,' murmured Olga, lost in thought.

'It's a shame! I'd reserved a table for the three of us at the Rivoli for tonight,' lied Aurtova, adding:

'But your Vostyach has a hard day ahead of him tomorrow! He'll have a huge audience. It's no bad thing he's taking it easy.' The professor glanced in the rear-view mirror to gage the effect his winning words were having.

'Poor fellow! Let's hope he doesn't take fright – he's not used to crowds,' said Olga, clearly preoccupied.

Aurtova did not answer, then, as the car turned into the Pohjoisesplanadi, he said encouragingly:

'Come on now, don't worry. Someone who's survived the gulag and is used to life in the arctic tundra will surely manage to put up with a bunch of fusty philologists. Anyway, tonight I have a little surprise for you'.

'A surprise?' she queried doubtfully.

'Tonight, Olga Pavlovna, on the occasion of the XXIst Congress of Finno-Ugric Scholars and by way of tribute to our longstanding friendship, I have the pleasure of inviting you to dinner at my cottage on the island of Vasikkasaari. The menu will be strictly Finnish!'

'Really, Jarmo, today it's one surprise after another. The last time you invited me to dinner was on your graduation day. Together with fifty others!' Olga was as startled as she was flattered.

'So at last I shall be able to meet your wife. Is she there already?'

'No, Margareeta is abroad, in Sweden. Visiting a sick relative, you know how it is,' replied Aurtova coldly.

'Oh, I hope it's nothing serious!'

Aurtova said nothing. He didn't intend to go into further explanations.

'But I've been so looking forward to meeting the saintly woman who has put up with you for fifteen years!' sighed Olga, in tones of false regret. After a brief pause, she added:

'Well, there will be other opportunities.'

'Oh, absolutely!' Aurtova reassured her vaguely.

They had now arrived outside the Torni. Aurtova parked the car and left the engine running.

'I'll take your case up to your room and see how Ivan's getting on. If he's awake, I'll ask him to come with us. He was so looking forward to seeing you,' he said, turning to face her.

A sudden look of tenderness stealing over her face, Olga nodded, and kept her eyes on the professor as he took her case out of the boot and proceeded cautiously to cross the icy road. At reception, Aurtova introduced himself as a taxi-driver working for the Yellow Line, and asked whether he could leave a case belonging to a certain Professor Boris Juknov, who would be arriving soon. Seeing the receptionist nod his head, an eager bell-boy in a red tunic picked up Olga's bag and put it behind the desk. While the professor lingered in the lobby, pretending to look for a number in the phone book, Olga, still seated in the car, was thinking. She was excited and unsettled by the prospect of spending an evening alone with Jarmo. She had always found him attractive, even if she had never been under any illusions that the feeling was reciprocated. Over the many years they'd known each other, he had never shown any romantic interest in her, not even when he got drunk at student parties; he'd never laid a hand on her, and the few times they'd danced together she'd been aware of a distinct wave of repulsion emanating from a handsome and overbearing man. Jarmo had always been a charmer, pursued and yearned after by many a beautiful woman. Olga was quite aware that she was plain. But, out of pride and spite, instead of making any attempt to remedy it, she cultivated her ugliness. She brazenly wore dresses that emphasized her ungainly figure. The fact that she had legs like a piglet was not going to come between her and fishnet stockings, nor did she have any qualms about tight trousers revealing her heavy buttocks. But, strangely, she felt that on that night something might be going to happen between her and her old fellow student, though she could not have explained why. Perhaps, because of some perverse fixation due to age, her body might at last have become attractive to an ageing womanizer. He'd had his way with so many lovelies, maybe the time had now come to sink his hands into the slack flesh of a faded spinster. Olga had no experience of such matters, but Jarmo's peek at the fold of her breast had not escaped her notice.

'No dice, he's sleeping like a top. I left the number of the Koirasaari Coastguard Station with the receptionist. If need be, they can come to the cottage and let me know.' Back in the car, Aurtova was rubbing his numb hands.

'Let's hope he doesn't wake up in the middle of the night and start playing his drum. He did do that once in Moscow, and I had trouble explaining to him that it's just not done,' said Olga nervously.

'He won't make any more noise than the discotheque over the road,' said Aurtova, pointing to a neon sign.

Olga was worried. She was about to ask if she could go up and take a peek at Ivan. She wanted to be sure he was all right. Even if she just caught a glimpse of him in the darkness of the room, she would be reassured by the sight of his small silhouette safely asleep on the bed. From the silence behind him, Aurtova sensed danger.

'Did he give you the pipe? Did you play it? He so much wanted you to!' she said after a pause.

Aurtova took the bone out of his pocket and put it between his teeth like a *kazoo*, turning towards her with a jaunty air.

Olga smiled, albeit unwillingly. She had an odd feeling that her host, too, was ill at ease. She felt gratified by the idea that Jarmo had set this whole thing up, prepared the supper, perhaps even ensured that Ivan would be asleep so that he could be alone with her. She forced herself to forget her worries and raised her shining eyes to meet Aurtova's gaze in the rear-view mirror. The professor, who knew a thing or two about women, lowered his chin and gave a sigh of relief. He went back on the attack with a new cheerfulness in his voice, adding:

'Well now, dear Olga! A groaning board awaits us across the frozen sea!'

The car skidded briefly and set off towards the port. This time, wanting to avoid going through Suomenlinna for a second time, he took the longer route, continuing to the sea at Tahvonlahti. There too a snowplough had opened up a track towards the islands, but there were no poles to indicate where it lay, only the traces of snow chains, sometimes obscured by heaps of wind-borne snow. When they had left the shore lights behind, Aurtova noticed that there were stars overhead. This did not help matters; he would have preferred the blizzard of a few hours earlier. Luckily, there was no moon.

Seated in the darkness, Olga listened to the thrum of the engine and the beating of her own heart. She stared out of the window at the snowy expanse as it loomed up before them in the glow of the headlights.

'At last we'll be able to talk a bit, just the two of us. Our meetings have always been so brief, at congresses and conferences. Then we don't see each other again for years. And to think that we once spent whole days together in the university library! These days I really know nothing about you,' she said, leaning forward over the seat so as to see Aurtova's face lit up by the green light of the dashboard.

'That's true. We lose touch and years go by in a flash,' he

said with a false sigh.

'You must admit, it's amusing that it should be the Samoyeds who always bring us together. Like in that special course we did. Let's see if you remember the name of the seminar where we first met.' Olga had placed her elbows on the back of the front seat and Aurtova could feel her breath on his neck.

'Aha! Now how could I forget that! "Cacuminal fricatives in Proto-Uralic", by Jove! A theory developed by that madman Collinder!' came the rejoinder, as Aurtova leant forwards towards the windscreen to put some distance between himself and her unwelcome breath.

'Well, that's always been your view. But a lot of us agree with him.'

'Oh, come on, Olga! That's all been done to death. Early Proto-Uralic could not originally have had predorsal-gingivals, apico-cacuminals and palatalized liquids all at the same time. What would a pack of hunters have done with three different types of el?'

'Not that old story again? Then how do you explain the postalveolar liquid found in Nenets, which is a synthesis of all three?'

'My dear, you know quite well that that's what's known as the principle of least effort. The sounds of a language tend to dwindle over time, perhaps because in every area of life men want to do as little as they possibly can. In their heart of hearts, they tend towards immobility, towards silence. Who knows, perhaps one day we'll all stop talking, and that will truly be the end of the world. Even you know that the older a language is, the more pared down its sounds will have become. The Quechuan languages have only three vowels. Chinese can express extremely elaborate concepts with the sound of just two notes. Take ideograms: originally they were orthographic signs, each brushstroke was pronounced separately. Now they have become petrified. One single ideogram is the equivalent to a whole speech.'

'What rubbish! The principle of least effort was called into question by Zipf as early as 1935. A sound which you find difficult to pronounce might be quite unproblematical for a Korean. Take nasals: the French wallow in them, but a Finn can't pronounce them even when he's got a cold.'

The shoreline of Vasikkasaari now came into view, with the outline of the cottage visible behind the snowy dunes.

'What an eerie place! Do you come here a lot?' asked Olga, peering towards the shadowy shore.

'I like to come here for the odd weekend. In the summer we use it as a holiday home. Margareeta likes picking berries in the woods, and I like fishing. In the evening we have a barbecue and sit talking in front of the fire. Whereas in winter Margareeta likes to stay in the warm in Helsinki and I come here to work. Solitude and silence, that's what a scholar needs!' came Aurtova's rather too glib reply.

'I didn't realize you were so fond of solitude and speculation. There was a time when all your fishing was done in the student hostel,' said Olga sarcastically.

'Those days are over,' said the professor, opening the car door for her with a smile.

'Those days are over,' Olga agreed, pulling the collar of her fur coat up around her ears.

Aurtova offered his guest his arm and escorted her to the door. Before leaving, he had taken the precaution of switching out all the lights in the cottage and turning the generator down to the minimum so as to save fuel. But he had left the fire alight, to ensure that the place would be reasonably warm.

'Goodness, it's nice and warm in here,' said Olga as she went in. At the back of the stove, some embers were still glowing. Aurtova poked the fire and added more wood. He lit the candles on the table and refilled the stove in the sauna. Then he went into the kitchen, put the wood grouse into the oven to cook and took the aperitifs and champagne out of the larder.

The candlelight etched deep shadows into Olga's face. She smiled brightly, her eyes following her host expectantly as he busied himself with his various tasks. Aurtova had noticed at the airport that Olga was dressed up to the nines. She was wearing large ear-rings, and a showy amber necklace hung in the décolletage of her silk blouse. She was also heavily made up: her mouth, smeared with too much lipstick, glistened greasily. Seated on the edge of the sofa, her hands in her lap, the Head of the Institute of Finno-Ugric Languages at the University of Saint Petersburg looked like a wistful housewife dressed up for a Saturday night out. Aurtova sniffed distastefully at the scent which was now beginning to waft through the warming air. He realized that he would have to give the room a thorough airing after she left.

'Tonight, as an hors d'oeuvre, the house is offering smoked salmon, followed by roast wood grouse and potatoes, with lemon sorbet as dessert. First, though, the aperitif: reindeer pâté, *piirakka* with rice, and champagne,' said Aurtova, putting the tray and bottle on the table.

Olga peered eagerly at the plate and turned her shining eyes upon her host.

'*Embarras de richesses!*'

'There's also a bottle of vodka outside the door. For reasons of neutrality, it is neither Russian nor Finnish, but Polish,' Aurtova added jokingly.

'An excellent compromise.'

'And, after dinner, a good soaking in the sauna.' He pointed towards the porthole at the end of the corridor.

'Oh, goodness! Naked, Finnish style? Will we be whipping

each other's back with fir branches?' asked Olga, blushing with excitement.

Aurtova nodded with a grunt. For him, that would be the hardest part of the evening. He was dreading it. But he hoped that the drink would work its magic: that the sauna would be the *coup de grâce* and that she would pass out, delivering him from the supposed climax. He poured them some champagne and raised his glass.

'To the Finno-Ugric languages!' he exclaimed.

'To the Finno-Ugric languages,' repeated Olga, They drank in silence.

'By the way, Jarmo, you haven't yet told me what you think of my Vostyach.'

Aurtova sat himself down in front of her as they sipped their champagne.

'Well, you were right, I must admit: I was deeply moved by the lateral fricative with labiovelar overlay. It's a sound that comes from the very depths of our history!' he said with feigned emotion. 'I imagine... I imagine you've brought the tapes with you? They will be invaluable material for the congress minutes,' he added meaningfully.

'Of course. I take them with me wherever I go, just to be on the safe side,' said Olga, patting the black leather bag hanging from her arm. 'In fact, I'd like to make a copy to take back with me to Saint Petersburg, for the faculty library. Can you see to that?'

'No problem, I'll have it done tomorrow,' Aurtova promised obligingly, staring at the bag as though it were a mirage, likely to recede before him at any moment. A sweet smell of resin was wafting through the room, and the heat was causing the furniture to creak as the grain breathed and expanded in the warmth. The fire was crackling cheerfully, lighting their faces up with its spurts of red. But their eyes remained hidden, sunk in the black cavities of their sockets. Each was seeking out the other's gaze in an attempt to read their thoughts. From behind his glass, Aurtova was observing Olga, who was nervously fiddling with her rings.

'As you probably know, some scholars in America claim that the lateral fricative with labiovelar overlay is also found in Palaic, or ancient Hittite,' Olga said suddenly, a hint of mystery in her voice. Aurtova took a sip of champagne, and made a clucking noise.

'Nothing could be more plausible!' he remarked, self-confidently. 'Just one more confirmation that the Indo-European languages were strongly influenced by Proto-Uralic. In ancient times we were the civilized ones and they were the barbarians. We were the masters, they were the slaves. Not for nothing is the word *aryan* so similar to the Finnic *orja*, which means slave.'

'Actually, we don't even know what Palaic sounded like – it's died out completely. I shudder when I think how many languages have met that fate,' said Olga, dreamily.

'Well, statistics tell us that one of the six thousand languages still spoken on this earth die out every two weeks, my dear,' retorted Aurtova, almost gleefully.

'And with each one that dies, a little truth dies with it,' Olga retorted in her turn, stiffening a little and rubbing her sweating hands.

'Whereas I would say the contrary is true: the fewer there are left, the more we're moving towards the truth, towards the pure language which contains them all,' said Aurtova, taking another sip.

'I once thought that way, too. Don't you remember when you hoped against hope to track down some speaker of Karagass among the Tungus?'

'The vanity of youth,' said Aurtova, shrugging his

shoulders. Olga shook her head. A burst of warmth caused her cheeks and ears to redden.

'The true meaning of things is hidden from us; it lies beyond the bounds of any one language, and everybody tries to arrive at it with their own imperfect words. But no language can do this on its own. Every single language is necessary to keep the universe alive,' said Olga ardently, giving Aurtova an impassioned look.

'A dying language is like a dying man. However unfortunate the death of any language, it's just a fact of life. While some will be born of it, yet others will die of it. Like men, words too have to adapt in order to survive. Those which burn themselves out, or move away from their original meaning, are doomed to disappear,' Aurtova noted coldly.

'But think what vast tracts of time each language has travelled though, how much it's said. And sometimes its survival or its extinction hangs by a thread! Do you know why the Vostyachs survived into the last century, while the Koibalics, the Motorici and the Karagass were already extinct by 1600?'

Aurtova had gone back into the kitchen to prepare the salmon hors d'oeuvre. He spread two plates with savoury biscuits, butter and gherkins.

'That I couldn't tell you,' he said from the other room. Olga went to join him, glass in hand.

'Because of an arrow, Jarmo. The Vostyachs invented a kind of arrow with side pieces. If it missed its mark, it would get stuck in the reeds, rather than lost in the swamps of the tundra. It was indeed one more arrow to their quiver: one more coot per day, enabling them to survive'.

'How intriguing! So it's an arrow I'll have to thank if I manage to prove that Helsinki was a Sioux Encampment and that I am a distant descendant of Jarmo Sitting Bull! Russian woman, never will you have my scalp!' said Aurtova jokingly. But the ironic note he'd tried to adopt stuck in his throat. Olga laughed, redder than ever, while her host refilled her glass.

'You're going too far, as usual, Jarmo!' she chided him in tones of affectionate reproach. Then she went on:

'It's true that Vostyach consonants open up new paths, but they have yet to be explored. All we can conclude from the discovery of Vostyach is that it is related to Eskimo-Inuit. At the time when the Indo-Europeans reached Europe, the Finno-Ugrians were migrating eastwards, and their linguistic unity was breaking up into various languages, increasingly remote from one another. But, without Vostyach, it was impossible to reconstruct this fragmentation. This is now within our grasp. As to your Finno-Ugrians, only one part of the Uralic branch went eastwards. Speakers of Veps, Ingrian, Estonian, Karelian, Sami and finally Finnish arrived in successive waves. That would also explain why you settled so far to the north: simply because the rest of the continent was already occupied. It's true that this will oblige you to reconsider your theories, Jarmo. But do you realize what fascinating new perspectives it will open up? Who knows, perhaps before too long we'll find ourselves together again attending a congress on the Algonquin languages of North America!'

Aurtova had been listening in silence, biting his lip in irritation. He uncorked the second bottle of champagne with an angry gesture.

'No, Olga, that's where you're wrong. The Finno-Ugrians were a single people, fragmented only marginally by the invasions of Altaic peoples who drove them westwards. A good idea of the various stages of our migration is given by the distribution of our languages across the map, between the Urals and the Gulf of Bothnia, and by their phonological development. To the east we have the *Dolichocephalics*, with indistinct or barely voiced consonants and some remnants of the *coup de glotte*. To the west, among the *Brachiocephalics*, the *coup de glotte* disappears and the consonants are clearer. Despite this dispersion, even today our languages are very similar, and still have all the sophistication of an ancient civilization. But during the Upper Proto-Uralic Period we were too far from the Mediterranean for anyone to notice us. There have been other ancient and sharp-witted peoples who, like ourselves, have thousands of years of history behind them. But they were at the centre of the known world: the Phoenicians, the Egyptians, the Hebrews. Like ours, the words of their languages are hard as slivers of diamond, they have been pared down to the bone by the pitiless scalpel of time. Then come the European peoples, currently at the height of their maturity. Their languages have a hard crust, but below it they are still soft. Then come the linguistic losers: stranded beyond the reach of history's flow, they are like linguistic ox-bow lakes. Some have already dried up, others will soon meet the same fate. They are peoples with wizened faces; they look like old sages who have seen it all, but inside they are still children, feral children whom no one has ever disciplined, who have grown up running wild, with no need to develop a sophisticated language. The sounds of their speech are too akin to the cries of animals. Your Vostyach is one of these. He does not utter words, but howls. Living alone among the beasts, his phonation apparatus has regressed. His velar and guttural consonants, for example, speak volumes: they are all posterior sounds made with the back of the mouth. According to Baudouin de Courtenay, producing sounds with the posterior phonatory apparatus is typical of animals. The dog, for example, barks with his larynx. Whereas man's phonatory development has led him to produce sounds with the front of his mouth, with his lips, with the tip of his tongue against his teeth and palate. It is the labials, the palatals and the sibilants which distinguish us from beasts. The language of your noble savage should be consigned to oblivion, not preserved. That's the truth of the matter! By freeing itself of Vostyach, mankind will be taking yet another step away from the animal kingdom.'

Olga shook her head in irritation. She helped herself to more smoked salmon and drained her fourth glass of champagne. Aurtova immediately refilled it, though he was beginning to see that it wasn't going to be so easy to get her drunk, and that he might have to resort to the green pills.

'Once, when we were at university, I remember you lending me a notebook, in which I found the following quotation from Znamensky: "All words are already present in reality, even before they have been uttered. They are like objects in shadow, which only the lantern of the mind can bring to light, one or two at a time, never all at once. There is no such thing as a dead word, because one word will constantly produce another, and all of them contribute to the meaning which the mind illuminates." That is a lovely image, a declaration of a love for language in all its forms. And you believed it, at the time. But today I can see that you are no longer the passionate scholar you once were. I feel that it is no longer languages which interest you, but something else – although I can't quite gather what that something is,' observed Olga bitterly. A whitish thigh became all too visible inside the black fishnet mesh when she crossed her legs.

'Well, today, with a good modern electric language, a sort of linguistic halogen lamp, you would be able to see the words Znamensky mentions all at once, and sweep the room clear of the dry bones of dead language,' joked the professor, once more taking his distance. 'Come on, Olga! Must everything always end so tragically when you Russians are involved? We just have different views, that's all it is. Let's just agree to disagree and enjoy the evening!' protested Aurtova, shrugging.

'You're quite right, why choose today to argue? We'll have plenty of time for that tomorrow. Tomorrow we'll be two linguists separated by opposing theories. Today we're two old friends from university, meeting after a long gap. Give me some wine, Jarmo, it's cold tonight,' said Olga, pretending to be cold and inching along the sofa towards her host.

'Of course! The wood grouse should be cooked by now,' he said, getting up in a hurry, and returning with a steaming pot he set down on the table. Savouring the rich smell, Olga winked at him and surreptitiously undid another button of her blouse.

The faces of the customers seated at the tables of the Café Engel glowed in the warm candlelight. It melted the snow from their hair, causing it to drip down from the brims of their hats. Even from outside the window Margareeta thought she could smell the fragrance of the cinnamon cakes, the violet pipe-smoke, the damp fur caps, the lavender-scented wax, even the bitter smell of newsprint: all smells which reminded her of Jarmo, that winter Sunday when she'd first met him, in this very place. This evening, though, wandering around through the snow-bright streets in search of her ex-husband, places she'd seen a thousand times, looked at indifferently for years, suddenly presented themselves cloaked in an aura of foreboding. Forgotten memories now rained down upon her, merciless as X-rays, revealing things she had tried to forget for years. Now she remembered smiles and glances that had escaped her at the time, the ticking of the clock in the living room, the signature tune of a radio programme and Jarmo still not home; a car door banging shut in a car park, the sound of high heels fading into the distance, Jarmo emerging panting from a street corner. Now, and only now, in that evening darkness, Margareeta unravelled any number of small mysteries, making connections between them, one by one, and constellations of shoddy actions, galaxies of lies took shape in the dark skies of her memory: a densely tangled web of all the low tricks of which Jarmo had been capable. Jarmo: there had been a time when even saying his name had filled Margareeta's heart with joy. Perhaps one should never fall in love in winter. Perhaps emotions were a bit like plants: they needed the spring to put down roots, the summer to flourish and produce their fruit, the autumn to prepare for the thankless season of dark and cold, when the sun is the merest memory. But her life with Jarmo had been one endless winter, a dry trunk which had never put forth leaves. Margareeta did not want to go into the Café Engel, she did not want to stir up other painful memories from the dank places where they lurked. But it was too cold to wait for him outside. She pulled herself together, tugged at Hurmo's lead and went back into the town centre, in search of an empty bar where she could drink, and mourn. She went back to Liisankatu for the umpteenth time, stood under Jarmo's window. But all the lights were out, and his car, parked in the street, lay under an even deeper layer of snow. Suddenly it occurred to her that Jarmo might be in his office. Of course, why had she not thought of that sooner? The congress on Finno-Ugric languages was about to start, and he would surely be in the university, putting the last touches to his paper. Margareeta cast an angry glance in the direction of the building next to the cathedral. The fourth-floor windows were dark, but she thought she saw something moving in the dark eye of one of them. Digging her heels firmly into the hard snow, Margareeta crossed the square and pushed open the big wooden door. She was well-known to the porter as Professor Aurtova's wife. He told her that her husband hadn't been in that Saturday; the last time he had seen him had been the previous night.

'He dashed off like the wind, scarcely even said goodbye,' he remembered, scratching his forehead underneath his peaked cap. Then he added:

'I haven't seen him today. Actually no one has been around. They're all in the conference centre.'

'I'm just going up for a moment to collect something,' said Margareeta, biting her lip.

'By all means! In fact, could you take this up for me?' said the porter, handing Margareeta a folder secured by an elastic band. 'The man who deals with the mail doesn't come in on Saturdays, and with my bad leg I have trouble with all those steps.'

Margareeta took the folder and set off up the stairs, switching on the light on each landing as she went. The Institute of Finno-Ugric languages occupied the whole of the fourth floor. There was only one light on in the corridor, above the photocopier. Hurto slithered over the gleaming parquet. Margareeta felt a sudden uprush of anxiety as she pushed open the door bearing the brass name-plate 'Prof. Jarmo Aurtova', and was surprised by a burst of cold air. She fumbled for the light switch. She had been right: what she had seen from down below had been the curtains billowing in the wind in front of the open windows. The Karelian carpet and the seats of the two Gustav II-style chairs were covered with a thin layer of snow, which had melted beneath the radiators, leaving two fan-shaped pools of water. All there was on the desk was a burnt-out candle and a bottle of cognac. The floor was glittering with shards of broken glass, together with the odd sheet of paper, blown about by the wind. Hurmo tugged on his lead and scratched at the parquet flooring, sniffing out his master's smell. Margareeta felt downcast, indeed alarmed. She let go of Hurmo's lead and clutched the folder to her as though it were a defensive shield. She walked around the room, looked behind the cupboards and under the desk, expecting at any moment to stumble upon her husband's frozen corpse. She closed the windows hastily and stood there, listening. The clock was ticking on its shelf, the small pair of gold scales was catching the milky light of the lamp. Big drops of water were falling from the curtains on to the sopping carpet. Down in the square a tram was rattling by. Breathing heavily, Hurmo was looking at his mistress with the same professorial look as her husband adopted when he was seated at his desk. Margareeta sighed, picked up the lead and hurried out of the room, along the corridor and down the stairs, tossing the folder on to the porter's desk as she passed it. He raised his eyes and watched her in bewilderment as she left the building.

Outside the conference centre, small vans were skidding over the ice in their attempts to reach the open space in front of the main entrance. Well muffled-up, workmen were unloading rolls of red carpet and laying them on the steps, fixing them in place with gleaming brass rods. In the main hall, which smelt of glue and paint, electricians were installing the microphones, testing the projectors and putting the finishing touches to switchboards full of coloured cables, like costly jewel boxes. Margareeta picked her way between men in green aprons arranging flowers and plants at the foot of the podium, cast her eye over the entrance hall, went to the floor above and tried the door handles of the various offices, to no avail, then peered through the glass spyholes. There was no one in any of the rooms; desks and hatstands were empty, cupboard doors closed. In the silent corridors, all that could be detected was the stale smell of a cigarette long since abandoned in a distant ashtray. Margareeta went back wearily down the stairs. Almost stock-still for once, Hurmo was waiting for her, well out of the way of the bustling workmen. He was panting, a gobbet of slobber permanently suspended from his tongue. He lifted his gaze to his uneasy mistress, who once again snatched up his lead bad-temperedly and dragged him after her, causing him to yelp. In the main hall, beneath a large panel depicting a Proto-Uralian rock carving, a cleaner was giving the last seats a half-hearted wipe.

'I think something has happened to my husband,' said Margareeta anxiously to the policeman who was putting the lid back on his coffee thermos.

Rauno Hyttynen had heard that phrase before. He pulled a form out of a drawer and started where he always started from: name, surname, address. Margareeta answered his questions patiently.

'To tell the truth, he's actually my ex-husband,' she added for further accuracy after some hesitation, fixing the policeman with a trusting look. But when Rauno Hyttynen handed her a copy of the report about the disappearance of the Finnish citizen Jarmo Aurtova and turned his back on her, to go and sit down in front of the television, Margareeta looked at him blankly.

'But... what are you doing? We must go straight to my husband's flat! I've been looking for him all day. I found the windows open in his office, and paper and glass strewn all over the carpet. Does that strike you as normal?'

'Madam, the first patrol to get here will take care of things. I'm on my own, and I can't budge,' he told her, tuning in to channel 1. The hockey match between Helsingfors Idrottsföreningen Kamraterna and Lokerit wasn't due to begin for fifteeen minutes, but preliminaries at the rink were already under way.

'And when will the first patrol be here?'

'Ah, that depends on where they've gone to watch the match,' said Rauno Hyttynen with a snigger.

'But something serious might have happened to my husband,' objected Margareeta fretfully.

'Madam, if whatever it is has already happened, it's too late. If whatever it is hasn't already happened, I can assure you that for the next two hours nothing at all is going to happen anywhere in Helsinki. Come back in two hours, and we'll find whatever it is that's gone astray: husband, stolen car radio, drunken grandfather or missing cat,' the policeman shot back wearily without taking his eyes off the line-ups of the teams which were now appearing in double exposure over the image of the pitch.

'But he might have had an accident! He might have been taken ill at home! He might have fallen into the sea! He might have been killed!' protested Margareeta, who in her heart of hearts hoped that all four of these disasters might somehow have befallen him at one fell swoop.

'He might also be at the rink, watching the match. And anyway, didn't you say he was your ex-husband?' the policeman retorted brusquely, turning up the volume.

Margareeta gave a sharp tug on the lead and stomped up to Hyttynen behind his desk.

'Officer! You see this dog?' she shouted, lifting Hurmo up by his collar and hurling him clumsily in the policeman's direction. Hurmo squealed, dug his claws into Hyttynen's thighs and brushed against them with his snout, leaving a trail of slaver on his trousers.

'Have a good look. He's just like my ex-husband.' Margareeta had taken Hurmo by the snout and was shaking him by the jaws, pressing him up against the horrified policeman. 'He walks like him, he sighs like him, at night I can hear him snore like him, even the stench of his wet fur smells like my husband's wet socks! Do you know how much longer an animal like this can live? Another ten years, that's how long! And I don't intend to spend another ten years taking my ex-husband to the park each evening for a pee, washing him in anti-flea shampoo every two weeks, taking him to the vet when he's on heat, buying him Pappy at the supermarket and giving him worming powder when – well, I'll say no more. So, kindly get up from that chair, because by this evening I intend to be rid of this animal, of my husband and of fifteen years thrown down the drain!' concluded Margareeta, beside herself with rage. Hurmo snarled half-heartedly and went to take refuge under the table.

Rauno Hyttynen saw that he was dealing with a trouble-maker; one of those busybodies who write indignant letters to the papers, complaining about police negligence. She might also be hysterical, and if things got worse he might have to take her to the accident and emergency department and give all manner of explanations. He dried his spittle-flecked hands on his trousers and walked backwards to take his jacket from the hatstand. He gave a last regretful glance in the direction of the television; at that moment it was showing advertisements, then there would be a newsflash; then the match would start.

'All right, all right. Let's go and see where your ex-husband has got to. But I can't do more than open the door to his flat,' said the policeman, tightening his belt. If he got a move on, with luck he might be able to see at least half of the hockey match he'd been looking forward to for a whole month.

Sirens blaring, they arrived in Liisankatu. Alarmed by the

unaccustomed commotion, the neighbours peeked through their curtains at the blue flashes slithering over the façades of the houses.

The neighbour who had opened the main door to Margareeta that afternoon now appeared on the landing: 'No one's at home. I haven't seen the professor since yesterday. The only person I've seen today is Noora,' she volunteered, giving her a sideways look as she noticed the policeman, and warding off an intrusive Hurmo with her foot.

'Police!' announced Hyttynen brutally, knocking loudly before turning the lock to Aurtova's flat with a skeleton key. When the door swung open, Hurmo rushed in, barking excitedly. Everything was in perfect order: the bed was made, the washing-up had been done. The cleaner had evidently been, because the shower mat had been hung up neatly, a pile of ironed shirts lay at the foot of the bed and a pair of slippers had been placed side by side in the shoe cupboard.

'I told you so. Your ex-husband has gone to a bar to watch the match!' said Hyttynen with a smile, raising his arms to propel woman and dog towards the balcony. Biting her nails in her anxiety, Margareeta thrust the policeman aside and proceeded to scrutinize every corner of the flat in search of some sign, some clue that might put her on Jarmo's trail. It was the first time she'd been into the furnished flat her husband had gone to live in after their divorce. She walked heavily through the sparsely furnished rooms, inspected the anonymous furniture, the slightly sagging sofa, the Ikea table with the price tag still around one leg, the faded poster of an old view of Helsinki. Then she went back into the hall and gathered herself together with a weary sigh. She pressed the button on the answerphone, which told her that there had been twelve messages, but they were all the unanswered ones that she herself had made. She opened the drawer in the small table below the mirror in the entrance hall, where she knew he kept the key to the garage. Hyttynen pulled a wry face, nodded impatiently and set off for the stairs.

'I've got to be getting back to the station,' he announced brusquely, lifting up the sliding door to the garage. Hurmo rushed into it, tail wagging furiously. Margareeta cast a sad look at the rolled-up blue tent, the canoe, the racing bikes, the old wooden skis: all familiar old friends which had made regular appearances in her life over the last fifteen years. She stepped on something on the ground which made a crunching sound, then shattered into bits of coloured plastic. She bent down to pick them up. The object in question was bait, the kind used for trout fishing. What was bait doing on the floor of the garage in mid-winter? Margareeta cast an eye over the assorted clutter in search of the box of fishing-tackle and saw it open on the table. She rejoined Hyttynen who was waiting for her at the door, fuming and stamping his feet.

'Officer! We must go straight to Vasikkasaari!' she informed him.

The Laplander started nervously when he met a police car going down Koirasaarentie. What would have happened if the engine had died on him there in the middle of the traffic? What if they'd stopped him for a police check? He'd brought along his pistol; he put his hand in his pocket to assure himself that it was there. If anything had gone wrong, he would have had no option but to fire. Over the last few miles before Tahvonlahti he had dreamed up the most catastrophic scenarios. He had imagined himself running across the frozen sea pursued by police dogs, a helicopter hovering above him, beaming a light down on to him, a loudspeaker ordering him to give himself up, both events being in fact thoroughly unlikely to occur on the shores of the Miekojärvi, rimmed by white birches and placid beaches. It was a relief to see the tourist harbour of Koirasaari coming into view. He went along the coast road in search of a steep slope, well away from the houses, then stopped and turned the engine off. He went over every detail yet again in his mind to be sure that he had not forgotten anything. He had taken care to remove all items of Katia's clothing that might lead to her identification. Beneath her long fur-lined coat he had dressed her as a prostitute, with fishnet stockings and a red bra, but without her rings, necklaces and watch. All her pockets were empty, except for the one where he had put the *koskenkorva*; he'd even poured as much as possible of it down her throat. All he had to do now was to throw her body into the sea. The police would assume that she was one of those drunks who lose their way after a hard night's drinking, fall down unconscious in the snow and freeze to death. Finland's graveyards were full of people who had met just such a death. Dragging Katia's body over the snow, the Laplander could not resist the temptation of looking into her eyes. She in her turn seemed to be looking back at him, reproachfully, as though he were to blame for her grim fate. The tree trunks he would fish out of the mud along the Miekojärvi had never looked at him in that baleful way; they never complained when he sank his hook into their bark. They were extremely biddable, gliding over the water to rejoin the others in the prevailing current. Panting with fear and exhaustion, the Laplander laid the dead body on the quay. He listened carefully, looked round him yet again and eased her towards the water with his foot, then heard a dull thud, followed by the sound of shattering ice. Then silence. He got back into the car and drove off, with no headlights, among the darkened houses of Varisluodonakar.

The very thought of Olga naked caused his stomach to go into knots. But his country was calling him to come to its aid, and the professor's thoughts turned with a flood of gratitude to the portrait of Mannerheim hanging in his study. The great marshal had done much more to save Finland than seduce an ugly Russian! Proceeding furtively into the kitchen, Aurtova crumbled three green pills into a glass of vodka and placed it on a tray beside a glass of water. He added two slices of lemon, hoping they would mask the cloudy colour of the mixture. Back in the changing room, he looked for Olga through the sauna porthole, praying he would find her unconscious, only to hear the sound of laughter, and the sight of her feet moving through the smoky air. Sighing with disappointment, he put the tray down on the small wooden table next to the deckchair and began reluctantly to undress, gritting his teeth with rage. He took the glass of vodka in his left hand, and the glass of water in his right. He took a deep breath and went into the sauna as though it were a gas chamber. Olga had drunk as much as he could have hoped for, but there was just no way of getting her drunk. Three bottles of champagne, four of cabernet, even half a bottle of vodka, and still she was holding out. Perhaps because she was biding her time, sensing that Jarmo was expecting something from her, and soon. Now she was stretched out on the bench, her eyes shining, giggling inanely and humming some song that she was clearly having difficulty remembering. The fantasy of carnal bliss was keeping her on the *qui vive*, ensuring that her every muscle remained alert and taut. Naked and sweating, she was twisting and turning like an animal on heat. She felt her body secreting previously unknown juices, her skin creeping beneath drops of sweat as they trickled over it like so many caresses. Clearly aroused, she was looking at her breasts and stomach, already imagining Aurtova's smooth white hands as he fondled them. She was trying to imagine how he would take her, whether on her knees on the hard bench or stretched out on the silk sheets of the bed she had glimpsed in the next-door room. Now she had settled down more comfortably on the cabin floor, as though in readiness for what must come. But even then she was babbling of Proto-Uralic phonetics, as though repeating some speech which had been endlessly interrupted.

The professor put the glass of vodka with the sleeping pills on a nearby shelf and went to sit on the other bench. In all the time he'd known her, Aurtova had never looked at Olga in the way a man looks at a woman. It was as though he was afraid of getting caught up in her ugliness, having it imprinted on his memory, unable ever to shake it off. Now on the other hand he would have to look at her fairly and squarely, fix his gaze firmly on that flabby, shapeless body, touch it, smell it. Olga was certain that this was indeed what the old Casanova wanted, and she did not want to disappoint him. She would not lose consciousness before yielding to his embrace. Only the sleeping pills could save Aurtova from his awful fate.

'Your national fixation with nudity turns out to be rather enjoyable!' she giggled, breaking into a gale of silvery laughter.

Seeing Jarmo come into the room, she had turned over on to her stomach and was waving the firwood branch that Jarmo had broken off for her from a tree.

'So, what are you waiting for? Surely you're not expecting me to whip myself?' She was pulling the green branch over her own back, and her voice sounded slurred. The shape of the bench had imprinted itself on her big buttocks, and she was peering at him from over her shoulder. Aurtova said nothing. He sat down as far away from her as he could, then put his elbows on his knees and scratched his chest.

'It's true, people take themselves less seriously when they see each other naked. Now I can see the white hairs on your groin, and that spare tyre, I'm much less in awe of you,' she added, coughing rather than laughing. She reached up, took the glass from the shelf and drank from it, eyeing her host's stomach with swollen, wine-befuddled eyes.

Suddenly embarrassed by his nakedness, Aurtova lowered his gaze. Olga was ready, impatient even; but she did not know how far Jarmo intended to push that particular game. The supper, the wine and then the sauna were all a build-up to something which was by now inevitable, but which Jarmo was postponing. Perhaps he was performing some propitiatory rite of seduction of his own making, some rigmarole which had to be rigorously respected in order for everything down there to proceed as it should. Presumably, for the experienced seducer, pleasure was to be approached by twists and turns. Perhaps the sauna was somehow a sacred place, and Olga would be able to enjoy her host's favours only when stretched out on the bed. Or perhaps, seeing her naked, Jarmo had quite simply had second thoughts, his curiosity about the wizened spinster doused by the sight of her sagging flesh. Olga did not know which of these possibilities was the more likely, but she was sated with pleasure as it was. She turned towards her old colleague, forcing him to look at her. That was her way of possessing him. One day, she liked to think, embracing one of the lovely women with whom he habitually surrounded himself, Jarmo would remember her own drooping breasts, her yielding flesh. Then the perfect body he was enclasping would slowly decay before his very eyes, would become shapeless and swollen until it became her own, that of the ill-favoured Olga Pavlovna.

'This too is a language, my dear Jarmo. Not one pronounced using the laynx, or the palate. Not one you write, or read, or need to learn, yet spoken the world over.' She raised a foot, finished off the vodka and continued:

'Indeed, maybe you Finns invented the sauna for this very purpose. Because, when all is said and done, it's only in a sauna that you can start to relax, to speak. With your bodies, not with words. A language like yours, which has so few liquids and occlusives and not one single palatal-fricative, does not exactly send the senses reeling; it does not put fire in your bellies.'

Wearily, Aurtova sought the right words to rebut this claim. That was how it had been throughout the evening – linguistic bickering. They'd been incapable of broaching any other topic.

'No, Olga, that's not true. For the Finns, the sauna is a place of utter chastity. Besides, we're not like you Russians, who hurl yourselves at anything that moves!' said the professor distantly, sipping his cold water.

At those words, casting all modesty to the winds, Olga looked up and adopted a less than decorous pose. The professor tried to avert his gaze from the crease that was all too visible between her wobbling thighs, but some malign force was keeping his gaze trained masochistically in that direction.

'For us, seduction means being able to talk to one another. For us, emotion is paramount; and nothing can stir our emotions more powerfully than well-chosen words. For Russians, don't forget, God is a verb,' warned Olga solemnly.

Aurtova was having trouble breathing. The heat was taking his breath away, draining him of all emotion. He had thought that he would be able to put the finishing touches to his plan with an unbearably hot sauna, but now it was he himself who was suffering. Defiantly, he threw a bucket of water on to the brazier, unleashing a burst of sizzling steam.

'We on the other hand are a people of few words. But our words have remained permanently frozen, like the arctic ice. Perhaps that is why we've managed to stand up to you, why we have never been drowned out by the Slavic tide: by using our sounds sparingly, transmitting them intact from generation to generation, honed by use. Your sounds on the other hand are blunted and round, like stones in a river. They have become shapeless, and your mouths skitter over them, unsure as to how they should be pronounced!' exclaimed Aurtova, waving a finger as though making some ex-cathedra pronouncement.

'Your language has never known the dizzying heights of universality. No one studies it, and all you can do is to repeat it among yourselves, because it tells of a tiny country no one knows. To communicate with the rest of the world you have to learn another one, you have to venture out among words which are not your own, which you have borrowed from others. Like second-hand clothes, they are not tailormade for you. They are too loose, or too tight, faded from use; they turn you into perpetual refugees. Whereas our language can tell of the whole world, and we can speak it from here to the Pacific. Thousands of foreigners study it, and in doing so they become steeped in our thought; the sounds of our language stamp the mark of our minds on theirs, conquering them as they do so. Our language is translated into a hundred others. A hundred other peoples want to understand us, and invent words in their own language which express our truths.'

Waving her arms around in her enthusiasm, Olga's face had turned scarlet. Aurtova was staring in disgust at the black bumps that were her nipples, at her sweat-streaked skin, at the locks of hair now sticking to her neck. He breathed in as deeply as he could, swallowing a mouthful of that moist, lifeless air, drenched with her cloying scent and sweat.

'Translation causes a language to become soiled; like blood in a transfusion, which is gradually tainted by impurities. Your language is a phial of blood on a hospital shelf, a curdled mass of random droppings. Ours on the other hand is a young vein, full of life, the fruit of a single body. By being translated, a language picks up meanings which are not its own, which infect it and poison it, and against which it has no defences. It is like the native Americans, who were wiped out by European diseases. Today they are almost all dead, their languages so many unpronounceable relics, tangled heaps of sound which no alphabet could ever unpick.'

Olga raised her eyebrows in displeasure. Aurtova could make out the damp white blotch in front of him increasingly dimly in the cloudy air, and this at least afforded him some relief.

'Easy now! Think twice before insulting the Indo-American languages: it might turn out that you're related. Did I tell you that my Vostyach barbecues beavers without skinning them? Just as the now vanished Potowatomi used to do in Canada! As to your beloved Finnish, aren't you forgetting that it is one of the few languages in the world without a future tense? And where can you hope to go without a future? Little by little, you'll die out. Because one fine day you won't even be able to tell each other what you're doing tomorrow.'

Aurtova wiped away the sweat that was trickling down his forehead and returned to the matter in hand.

'It is you who have no future! Just look at you, weary of yourselves and of the world, almost complacent about the rancid smell you give off. Too much history has worn you out. Tomorrow I shall prove that your Vostyach is just a mentally handicapped member of the Nganasan group with problems of articulation,' he said, wagging a finger threateningly in Olga's direction.

'The force of his words will be my Vostyach's most powerful defence. Did you know, in Vostyach *powakaluta* means "something grey glimpsed vaguely running in the snow". That may strike you as funny, indeed it seems scarcely credible that a language should have a word for such a concept.

109

We don't even know what this grey thing is. But, when the Vostyach language disappears, *powakaluta* will vanish with it. Or rather, there will still be something grey glimpsed vaguely running in the snow in the Siberian tundra, but the word to describe it will no longer exist. And that is terrible, and certainly has something to do with God!' said Olga forcefully, raising her eyes; and when she raised her arms as well, her breasts wobbled like jellies, then slapped back stickily on to her stomach.

Aurtova was panting with the heat. Now his whole body was beginning to feel inexplicably itchy, so that he had to tie himself in knots to scratch himself. He looked at the red blotches which had suddenly bloomed on his chest and stomach: all manner of hideous diseases came to mind. This waiting was beginning to take its toll. He felt a grim desire to hurl himself at Olga and pummel her into silence. But he managed to restrain himself, forced himself to relax and protested mildly:

'Come on now, Olga, enough of these ramblings. When we came in here this evening we made a non-aggression pact, but you refuse to bury the hatchet. So don't try telling me that *I'm* the Indian! Surely the idea was to move on from linguistics and talk about ourselves?'

Olga burst into genuine laughter. She pressed her knees together, took hold of the fir branch as though it were a bunch of flowers and settled herself comfortably, giving Aurtova an appeasing look.

'You've always been extremely likeable, Jarmo. Handsome and likeable. That's why everyone always forgives you for your loutish behaviour. Yes, you're right: let's talk about us! Tell me where your wife's gone off to. This business about a relative in Sweden just won't wash. Tell me why you brought me here this evening, why you wined and dined me and got me to take my clothes off,' she said, with a sudden tenderness. But Aurtova was quick to change the subject.

'First let's see whether you are up to a roll in the snow. Come on, I'll race you to the shore and back. The winner will get another glass of vodka.' Even as he proffered the challenge, Aurtova was still clinging to the dwindling hope that her timely collapse would spare him the evening's by now inevitable conclusion.

'You've got yourself a bet!' said Olga, heaving her massive body down from the bench.

Outside, it was pitch black. The distant lights of the city were almost lost beneath the heavy, louring sky. Out to sea, the waves were taking on the ghostly forms of a vast cavern, bristling with stalagmites, strewn with craters and crests as black as lava, concealing measureless chasms. Intending to lose this absurd race, Aurtova allowed himself to be overtaken, running clumsily out of the trees and, reaching the beach, pretending to stumble in the snow. He could just make out the mass of her gummy white body in the faint starlight as she overtook him. When he went back into the cottage, his body was aching and steaming with cold. When he caught sight of his puny white frame reflected in the glass of the veranda, he felt a sudden pang of weakness. Panting, he followed Olga's damp footsteps into the changing room, then went into the sauna to warm up. Hunched up against the stove, he realized he had a fever: he was trembling all over, and his teeth were chattering. A stab of pain shot through his forehead. He thrashed his back and chest with the branch of firwood, hoping that would get his circulation going. The sauna was cooling down, he would have to get more wood, but was too weak to move. He felt his temples throbbing furiously. Behind them, an overburdened vein was beating wildly, sending blue flashes across his eyes. His limbs felt sluggish and he could scarcely breath. He fell to his knees, and in the hazy distance saw the wild horde of Pecheneg horsemen coming at him again, urging on their horses with short plaited whips and dragging bloody corpses through the dust, bouncing along like so many sacks. Soon they would be upon him. He could already see their gleaming leg-guards, their spiked helmets, the whites of their glaring eyes, he could hear their animal howls, the whinnying of their terror-stricken horses. He threw himself under the bench, covering his head with his hands, hearing the dull thud of the hooves on the ground. When he recovered consciousness, the room was in darkness, except for a feeble glow coming from the changing room. He did not know how much time had gone by, whether he had slept or fainted. He had pins and needles in his legs, his feet were frozen and his head run through by a thousand needles. He sat up, gathering his strength; propping himself up against the wall, he managed with one last desperate effort to get to his feet.

Stretched out on the bed, Olga drew the sheets up around her, excited by slight wafts of aftershave. Then she discovered the warm nest they came from, the silk pyjamas Aurtova had laid out on the pillow, and sunk her nose into them, rubbing the material so that it would release its scent. Without undoing it, she pulled the jacket over her bare flesh, pressing the soft pillows against her breasts. Suddenly she felt unable to breath, her limbs seized up in a spasm which shot through her like cramp, as draining as a fit of retching, but more long lasting. She was panting now, digging her nails into the foam rubber, when she saw a pinkish glow passing in front of the door and heard Jarmo's steps approaching. She kicked off the covers, pushed away the pillows, stretched out her arms and spread her still trembling thighs over the empty mattress. She waited to feel the candlelight warm upon her stomach, to have Jarmo's weight at last upon her, the smell of the living man there in her nostrils. But now she felt a new weakness slowly creep over her body, causing the spasm to melt away. Her breasts slackened, her knees buckled, her jaw relaxed, giving her lips back their usual expression of gentle sadness. Olga realized that she was sinking into unconsciousness, but by now nothing could matter less. Jarmo had been hers. In that bed. She had possessed him. No one would be able ever to deny it.

Once he had reached the changing room, Aurtova noticed that the lamps in the living room were flickering and becoming dim. They flickered a little longer, then went out. Now the room was lit only by the almost burnt-out candles on the table. Their faint light was casting shadows on the walls, those of the empty bottles, the smeared glasses, the congealed remains of supper glistening on the plates. The professor strained his ears for some sound of the generator, but it had gone out. He went into the hall, grabbed his jumbled clothes from the coatrack and put them on, feeling his forehead constantly as he did so. Fumbling in the darkness in the kitchen, he came upon the torch, then remembered that it had no batteries. He picked up a still guttering candle and found some aspirin in the medicine chest, swallowed down four tablets, without water, and began to grope his way around the house in search of Olga.

From the corridor, he glimpsed her in the bedroom, on the double bed. She looked like some beached whale, washed up on a river bank. He went into the room, saw that shocking black chasm looming out of the semi-darkness. He sniffed disgustedly at the animal sweat, mingled with the smell of alcoholic breath. Yet some perverse attraction drew him on to scrutinize the abomination from a nearer vantage point. A sudden shudder ran through Olga's blubbery frame. Aurtova drew back in alarm, seeking refuge in the gloom, but almost at once all movement ceased, and her body became as ominously motionless as before. Aurtova lifted the candle to peer at her face in its feeble light. She opened her eyes and smiled, as though waking up from some pleasant dream.

'You're so handsome, Jarmo! The older you get, the more handsome you become!' she murmured voluptuously before sinking back into unconsciousness. The professor gave a sigh of relief; he suddenly felt distinctly less unwell. He waited for a few moments, then shook her several times in a gingerly fashion, taking her by the shoulder with the tip of his fingers, as though afraid of sullying himself. But Olga did not stir. She was breathing more and more quietly, looking more and more unappealing. Shaking with fever, Aurtova crumpled on to the bed beside her and pulled the covers up. That had been a near thing. The sleeping pill had done its work at last. He stayed put, waiting there in the warm until some semblance of strength returned, keeping an ear out for sounds of Olga's increasingly faint breath. At last he felt strong enough to get up, fumbled around in the gloom, picked up her clothes from the chair and dressed her in them, in the light of the last candle-end, this time forcing himself to touch the spongy flesh more closely, because she had to be correctly dressed, not a hair out of place. He slipped her suit jacket over her silk blouse, zipped up her skirt, did up her belt – with difficulty – at the right hole and laced up her boots, making sure he got them on the correct foot. He didn't attempt to put on her jewelry, there was too little light to get her ear-rings in and do up her necklace properly. He put it into his pocket, wrapped up in her silk scarf. He found her fur coat in the hall and put that on her too, doing up all the fastenings. He found her black leather bag hanging from the bed-head and rummaged through it warily, until he came upon two tapes, which he put into the inside pocket of his jacket. He picked up all the bits and pieces lying on and underneath the bed, together with the bath robes which had been left in the changing room. He put the lot into the sheets, tied them up and put them in a jute sack. At that point the candle-end drowned in a pool of melted wax, so that now the only light came from the dying embers in the hearth. But Aurtova lay down on the floor and searched every inch of it, then every piece of furniture, every drawer, every nook and cranny to ensure that the cottage would bear no trace of what had happened there that night. He put the remnants of the supper, the glasses, plates, bottles and the little jar of green pills into another sack, together with the cooking pot and candlesticks. He doused the embers with a few handfuls of snow, and raked the ashes with the fire shovel. He checked the outside lumber room. Feeling for the generator in the dark, he saw that there was a split in the tank. That was why it had failed: the petrol had leaked away, making a puddle outside on the ice, which he concealed by covering it with fresh snow. Then he dragged Olga outside and laid her on the back seat of the car, together with the sacks, started the engine and drove, without the headlights, down to the shore, where the ice was hard and he would leave no trace. Then he went back and looked around the cottage, securing all the locks. He fixed the rubber watering hose to the tap in the lumber room and directed the jet upwards, using the hand pump. The water fell back on the ground like gravel, covering the tyre marks, and Olga's footsteps in the patches of snow along the shore. It proved time-consuming work. Finally he sprayed the doors and windows, which were instantly covered with glistening droplets. He put the hose back in the lumber room and walked in a wide circle on the ice, over the frozen sea, to go back to his car. He checked his watch: it was exactly midnight. He started up the engine and drove slowly to the quay at Koirasaari, still without turning on the headlights. He stopped near the ballast in the tourist port, where the tyre tracks of the snowploughs left their marks as they drove up from the beach. There he opened the car door and let Olga's body tumble out. He continued along the shore, beyond the lighthouse and back again on to dry land. At the first lights of Varisluodonkari he drew up at the verge and took off the chains.

While he was driving along the road to the airport, still dazed with fever, gripping the steering wheel as though it were the handle of a dagger, Professor Aurtova had a brief moment of lucidity. For an instant, his hectic mind was lit up by a flash of scientific spirit. He remembered the tapes he had in his pocket, and felt an urgent desire to listen to them, to hear the language once spoken by the now vanished Vostyachs. He turned on the radio and slipped the first tape into the lit-up mouth of the cassette player. Then, in the silence barely broken by the humming of the engine, the voice of Ivan Vostyach emerged from the surrounding cold as it had for the first time in the distant forests of the Byrranga Mountains. In all probability, thought the professor to himself with chilling nonchalance, that was the voice of a man already dead. Still, he felt a shiver run down his spine when he heard the lateral fricative with labiovelar overlay ring out loud and clear in the chill air. So, the mysterious semi-consonant of the American Indians had indeed been heard in Asia, too. It issued from the deepest entrails of mankind, perhaps indeed from those times immemorial when men had only just started to stand upright. Aurtova listened in astonishment as that ancient sound vibrated in his ears, as it was borne away on the icy wind which was its native home. It set forgotten follicles stirring in the soft pulp of his brain, disturbing liquids that had lain motionless for centuries, arousing sensations not made for men of the modern world. Stunned by what he had heard, befuddled by fever, Aurtova felt the car going into a sudden skid; the spiked tyres grazed the kerb and the headlights revealed a wall of birch trees. He slowed down and came off the motorway just before Vantaa, taking a track which went deep into the woods. He stopped in a clearing, turned off the lights and waited for the silence to close in again around him. Then he got out of the car, kneeled down in the snow and used his lighter to set fire to the two cassettes. The plastic sizzled and crackled, then shrivelled away, spraying the air with a fine rain of fiery ashes. All that remained of the voice of Ivan Vostyach was a sticky, evil-smelling little lump which soon hardened in the snow.

III

From the top of his icy dune, Ivan stared at the black linc which ran across the sea, branching out like a warm vein. Dragged by the strong current, the water was sending up a hail of spray; it was only near the shore that a slight, pearly white skin would form, to be shattered under the impact of the stronger waves. It was impossible to venture further out. Ivan had walked for miles, keeping clear of the last islands. He had advanced ever further into the desert of ice, following the eastern stars, those he could see shining beyond the woods from his mountains, towards the great river delta. He had clambered over huge clefts, sending the reindeer ahead of him, then pushing the sledge over the frozen surface to act as a footbridge. Around the islands most exposed to the wind, the sea had closed in, forming deep seams whose sharp peaks disfigured the frozen surface of the waves like scars. Ivan had had to split them with his axe to enable the runners of the sledge to clear them. But now he would have to turn back, because his way was barred, and skirting the flow of the current might be dangerous. Ivan turned towards the north. That was the only way of avoiding the city. He turned his reindeers' heads toward the constellation of Urgel and set off again. He was hoping to reach the thick woods he had seen from the train window on his arrival in Helsinki. The horizon was sucking the light out of the stars; they were falling to earth in countless numbers, crossing infinitesimal spaces but taking centuries to do so. Ivan hadn't taken his eyes off them since he had left Korkeasaari. He felt an unknown force closing in around him, and he was beginning to fear that it might be Ticholbon, the star which placed itself in front of the winter constellations and blocked their way. The old men of the Byrranga Mountains would drive it off with their axes, and their song. They would stay up the whole night staring at it, and in the morning people would find them in the forest, covered in ice but nonetheless triumphant. But you had to know just how to look at it: if you fixed it with an irreverent gaze, you might go mad. Ivan had heard tell of certain black shamans from the great river who had gone up into the mountains to drive Ticholbon away and who had found themselves destined to sing, hysterically, for the rest of their days. They were shunned by the villagers, who threw stones at them and made amulets of reindeer bone to ward off their spirits; even the wild beasts gave them a wide berth. That was why Ivan was fearful of lifting his eyes to the cold star, up there to the north-east, between Khaanto and Suolta.

When the icebreaker Sisu moved off from the quay at Pohjoisstama with a blast of its foghorn, the guanacos and wild goats galloped away in alarm. The crust of ice shattered before it with a sound of mangled stone, but it sailed serenely onwards, leaving a heaving strip of black water in its wake, wide as a road. It was going towards the open sea, to reopen the sea routes which crossed the Baltic. Soon its lights disappeared into the darkness, leaving a gleaming black chasm beside the quay where it had been moored, in which the buildings on the shore were now reflected like so many snaggleteeth. Now it was in the distance, buried beneath piles of cloud, and Ivan could no longer see it. But he felt the crust of ice swaying like a raft, and heard a roar, stronger even than thunder, explode in the open sea beyond the furthest islands. To the west of Lonna, the icebreaker had opened up a foaming trench giving free passage to the ferries to Tallinn. Now Ivan's route to the forests was blocked by an impassable abyss. Alarmed by the hubbub, he took the whip to his reindeer, heading them towards the city. The sledge hissed and bounced over the snow, which split like a pane of glass beneath its runners. Ivan tried to peer beyond his reindeers' straining necks to keep an eye out for the frozen clefts and mounds, and avoid the wind-hardened dunes. Fortunately, however, he had chanced on an expanse of unruffled sea, which had frozen over evenly, as though it had been stilled by the cold which rose up from the depths, and then been covered by a steady fall of snow. When he felt that he was out of danger, he got down from the sledge and bent down to listen. Now he could hear nothing, indeed see nothing, except, there in the distance, the faint glow of the city. There was nothing for it. He had to go that way in order to head eastwards. He drove his reindeer towards a heap of ice, put his drum on the ground and began to beat it with his scrap of bone. It ticked away in the silence like a mason's chisel, chipping away at successive rims of sky. Ivan looked towards the north. There it was, as tiny and sharp as a spark, below the dim halo of Khanto. It was barely throbbing, stuck like a thorn in the flesh of the night. But, at every breath it drew, all the other stars grew paler, because Ticholbon was soaking up their light. Only the distant southern stars were shining, untrammelled in the less crowded sky. Now Ivan was beating more loudly on the drum skin, which pulsed like a sheet of steel in the silent air. His breath, the course of the blood in his veins, the tautness of his muscles, everything within him was governed by that rhythm. He drummed until he could feel the very ice beneath his feet sending back the same beat, until the reindeer were still and even the wind died down, slithering almost noiselessly over the snow which was now giving out an eerie, opalescent light. Then, one after the other, the Vostyach sang out the five magic words of the black shamans. He picked up the axe and hacked fiercely at the crust of ice. Ticholbon sparkled. Ivan struck again, unleashing a rain of shards into the air, and then again, until, spark after spark, Ticholbon was thoroughly ablaze in the high heavens. It burned up in an instant, sputtering with a ruddy gleam and leaving a black patch in its place. Then all the other stars regained their light, took on new strength, breathed with new vigour, and slowly the starry vault began to turn once more. Now Urgel was free to go on his way, to lead the world out of winter's grip.

Listening to the hockey match on the radio was not the same thing as watching it on television, of that he was assured. Hyttynen tried vainly to picture the scrum at the second face off, and the powerful shot from the neutral zone which had again given the advantage to the Lokerit team. The commentator's excited voice reported every detail of the action, rattled off the names of the players as the ball passed from one to the other. But without being able to see the puck, and the sticks embroiled in hand-to-hand encounters, for Rauno Hyttynen, a fan of the Helsingfors Idrottsforeningen Kamraterna, the winter's most eagerly anticipated hockey match lost all appeal, as did the hundred marks he'd bet on the outcome with Lieutenant Lampinen. Disavowing the ethical stance to be adopted by any fan worthy of the name, Hyttynen even began to hope that there might be a draw, leading to extra time. With a bit of luck, he would at least manage to see that. But Vasikkasaari was still a long way off, and the minutes were ticking by on the dashboard clock. They had only just been through Suomenlinna, and the icy track was hardly conducive to fast driving. This woman must be really worried, thought Hyttynen, glancing at her out of the corner of his eye. He'd seen a lot of such rapidly ageing female intellectuals who were now at last waking up to the fact that it wasn't their brains that made them interesting. Their husbands soon got tired of them, dumping them as people did with dogs before going on holiday: slightly ashamed of themselves, but resolute. Talking of dogs, that shapeless creature which the woman dragged along with her smelt quite abominable. It had settled itself comfortably on the back seat and was panting, its tongue hanging out. It must be one of those indoor dogs, which have never seen a wood and eaten nothing but tinned food all their lives. Hyttynen was still not sure what it was that linked the animal to her ex-husband, but he was certainly not going to ask for further explanations of the woman seated beside him, who was fiddling with her rings and looking impatiently towards the sea. Of all the police stations in Helsinki, what dastardly stroke of ill luck had led her unerringly to his own? Rauno Hyttynen had been studying the work rota for weeks in order to ensure that he would be duty in the station on the evening of the match. Leave was out of the question, Palolampi had broken his foot and would be off all month. So Hyttynen had exchanged his February shift with Vennamo, so as not to be on evening patrol in January, and had come to an agreement with Donner that all evening calls would be diverted directly to the patrol car radio. That way he would be able to watch the match all on his own, in suitable peace and quiet. And all that manocuvring had been for nothing. The most important match in the whole championship was now on, and he would miss every single minute of it.

'Here we are!' said Margareeta when they arrived at the quayside in Vasikkasaari. Hyttynen switched on the driving beam. The track across the sea met up with the road beside the landing stage, where the ferry to the islands moored in summer. Now, though, it was trapped in a mass of ice shaped like some monstrous creature. Roosting on the wooden piers, it cast a black shadow over the stiffly curled waves. There was no sign of life on the island. The car tyres crunched loudly in the muffled silence of the woods. On the southern slope the trees were laden with snow, but as soon as the road started to run towards the promontory, and the coast, the car lights revealed mere skeletons of trees, like totem poles, which vicious winds had whipped bare of any remaining snow. The rocks on the shoreline were white and bare, like the stones of a lunar landscape. A huge snowdrift had piled up at the entrance to the lane leading to Villa Suvetar.

'Is Suvetar your name?' asked Hyttynen, reading out the words on the wooden nameplate on the gate in an attempt to appear pleasant, and thereby lessen her mulishness.

'No, it's the name of the goddess of summer,' snapped back Margareeta.

'Oh, excuse my ignorance,' said Hyttynen apologetically. He got out of the car and took a shovel and a torch out of the boot.

'The house is at the end of the lane,' Margareeta informed him, getting out after him.

Hyttynen huffed and puffed as he dug away beyond the gate, sinking into the snow step after step as he approached the house. He shone the torch on Margareeta and Hurmo, who were floudering along behind him.

'There's no one here, no footsteps, nothing,' he said, still vainly hoping that she might be persuaded to abandon their pointless search.

'Maybe not, but we've got to go inside,' shouted Margareeta breathlessly, stabbing her finger in the direction of the cottage door.

'The lock has frozen up. I'll have to go and get the anti-freeze,' said Hyttynen in irritation, letting the shovel fall to the ground. He came back a few minutes later, followed by

Diego Marani

Hurmo, who regarded him as one of the family by now, and sniffed confidingly at his every footstep in the snow.

On entering the cottage, Margareeta stiffened. Taking the torch from Hyttynen, she shone it into every corner, engaging on a search every bit as professional as his own.

'There's a smell of woman in here,' she muttered, nostrils flaring. Hyttynen looked at her in alarm: her eyes seemed positively to glitter in the darkness. Now not only would he miss the match, but the whole night might be wasted.

'Nonsense! It smells to me like lavender, the kind you put in drawers. People always put lavender in amongst the linen in cottages like this when they leave them locked up for the winter,' he added hopefully.

'No, that's the smell of a woman. A whore, in all likelihood,' insisted Margareeta, moving towards the sauna. She felt the boards and brazier, drew a hand along the bench and porthole in the door.

'Not a sign of dust!' she exclaimed triumphantly, then, turning to Hyttynen:

'Officer, call the criminal laboratory – now!'

'Madam, you surely can't be thinking of opening an inquiry just because your husband has a cleaner who makes a proper job of things? This is the limit, I've got to get back to the station, I've been patient quite long enough!' he protested, thrusting Margareeta unceremoniously out of the door, locking up in a somewhat slipshod fashion and setting off towards the car, noting with irritation that Hurmo was close on his heels, tail wagging furiously.

'I'm quite certain that someone has been here, and that they'll be back again before dawn!' Margareeta shouted, but Hyttynen had now vanished into the darkness. She waited for the torchlight to disappear among the trees, then walked around the house and down to the shore where, not so much earlier, a naked Olga had run to meet her fate. She stopped at the puckered sea, surprised at not hearing the sound of the undertow. Distant summer afternoons now came into her mind, Hurmo running in the sand and hurling himself into the water to swim up to the boat, Jarmo jokingly scolding him because he'd driven off the fish. It seemed impossible that this could be the same place: looking at the surrounding landscape, Margareeta suddenly felt that no summer would ever come to melt that ice again, that Villa Suvetar and all her memories would lie fossilized beneath it for all eternity. In the smudged grey sky above Helsinki a few pale greenish stars could just be seen; in the other direction, though, towards the open sea, they shone out more strongly in the total darkness. Straining her ears, beyond the sound of the fitful wind she heard a faint creaking spreading over the gauzy mass of ice: it was as though the whole sea had become an immense meadow peopled by insects which had congregated to launch a dawn attack on Helsinki. Swept northwards to those bleak latitudes by some natural disaster, they would cover the streets and houses of the city with a swarm of green snow. Made sluggish by the cold, they would soon die, flitting around clumsily before freezing to death and floating down to earth. Car wheels would reduce their sticky multitude to a pulp, leaving a stinking black mush on the asphalt. Margareeta imagined the headlines: 'After the big freeze, Helsinki is overrun by locusts.' She shook herself to clear her head of these mad imaginings, did up the top button of her windcheater and was about to make her way back to the cottage, when a dark shape bobbed up out of the sea and came to a halt in front of her. Margareeta drew back in alarm, but nonetheless peered in fascination at the shapeless mass which was coming towards her. Then she ran off towards the wood, slipping and falling in the snow as she did so. She was about to cry out, when two horn blasts rang out in the frozen air.

Then the four guanacos pricked up their ears and flared their nostrils, looked in four different directions and galloped off in fear, their little hooves ticking away on the ice until they receded into the distance, and silence fell again.

Aurtova swept grandly up the steps to the cathedral, then paused outside the main door to take in the length and breadth of the square. His mission was accomplished. Finland was safe once more. He thought back to every detail of that day, reviewed it again from start to finish to reassure himself that there was no possibility of any oversight. He had cleared everything up scrupulously, thrown the jute sacks over the railway bridge. He had gone to collect Olga's case from reception at Torni and put it in a locker in the left luggage office at the station, throwing away the key. He'd burned the tapes with the recordings of the Vostyach in the middle of the wood. He'd put Olga's jewels through some letterbox. He'd called by at his office to collect the paperwork for the conference, and the text of his own speech. He'd taken the hired car back to the airport and asked the taxi-driver to leave him in front of the cathedral, because he was in such a state of excitement that he couldn't even think of sleep. He needed to walk, to wear himself out in order to forget that endless night. Perhaps he still had a fever, but he was no longer aware of it. He felt thoroughly euphoric, but also nervous, and his blood was coursing wildly through his veins.

The silent square lay stretched before him like a deserted drawing room. He cast an affectionate glance in the direction of his office window, at the crisp architecture of the university colonnade, with the flight of steps leading up to the dark wooden main door, and the lighted windows of the Café Engel on the corner opposite, site of his many rendezvous and amorous conquests. At the end of the Unioninkatu, towards the sea, the chandeliers in the fashionable restaurant where he took all his meals were still ablaze. A little further on, beyond the silent barracks, was his modest, simple bedroom in the villa in Liisankatu. It was not there that he took his women, but to the grand hotels on the Esplanadi, where a suite, his favourite champagne and pairs of silken sheets, embroidered with his monogram, were permanently at his beck and call. For Professor Jarmo Aurtova, Helsinki was not just the capital of Finland, it was above all his personal apartment, its sumptuous rooms strewn among the city's streets and squares. That memorable January night Aurtova was simply strolling through his own home, checking that all was in order before going to bed.

Now the last trams were heading for their sheds, casting their fire-fly glimmer on the snow. The odd drunkard was waving his way home, keeping a cautious hand against the wall. The last of the Vostyachs would be in Sweden by now, lost for ever in the streets of an unknown city or perhaps already dead, and the only person who knew of his existence was lying frozen on the shore of an island in the middle of the Baltic. All Finland was lying curled up in its granite nest, unaware that it had just been plucked from danger. Aurtova walked towards the sea, then went along the Esplanadi, skirted the station and went up the avenue leading to the parliament building. He crossed the road and stood to attention in front of the equestrian statue of Marshal Mannerheim. The hero of Finland could rest easy in his bed. Now the Finnish language would never be linked to that of the wild Red Indians. Indeed, it would spread ever further eastward, wresting the former lands of the Proto-Uralian fatherland from the Slavs. The Algonquins would never put up their filthy teepees on the banks of the Pyhäjärvi. They would stay put, selling feather headdresses to tourists and getting drunk on their dismal reservations, gloomily waiting to become extinct. Aurtova looked tenderly at the austere figure of the old soldier, clicked his heels and performed a military salute. Then he put one hand on his chest and began to sing the national anthem. He saw the Pecheneg horsemen fleeing for their lives, vanishing into the misty steppe, throwing down their arms, retreating in terror as they did so, stumbling over the corpses of their fellows. Then they leapt on to their horses and unbuckled their breastplates in order to beat an even hastier retreat, pursued by the Finnish cavalry, swords drawn and unfurled banners billowing in the wind. Over the days which followed, the awestruck soldiers on guard in the Finnish army barracks told their incredulous superiors of how, in the depths of that polar night, the portraits of Marshal Mannerheim on the walls of the company offices, dormitories and corridors had lit up with the ghost of a smile. This was attributed to the extreme cold, the lateness of the hour and the excessive amount of cordial the recruits themselves admitted they had imbibed.

Still too agitated to think of sleep, Aurtova felt a sudden urge to pass by the Grand Marina Palace, where the XXIst Congress of Finno-Ugric languages was to open the next day. He walked down to the quay at Katajanokka, pausing to cast a respectful eye over the flags of the Finno-Ugric nations fluttering at the bottom of the steps. The wind was sending the ropes clattering against the flagpoles, causing the coloured cloth to snap sharply in the cold air. The whole of Katajanokka reminded him of a great ship, its sails unfurled so as to release it from the ice in which it was currently trapped. The professor practised climbing the flight of steps in a debonair fashion, as he would the next day. Reaching the entrance, he pretended to greet various dignitaries. He shook hands with ambassadors, paid his respects to their lady wives, kissing the hands of the lovelier among them. Then, fearing he might be seen by some night watchman, he hurried down again towards the quay. At last he was beginning to feel tired, and thought it might be wise now to go home. Thrusting his numb hands into his pockets, he came upon the little bone pipe Ivan had given him. He twisted it in his fingers, suddenly amused. He took it to his mouth, blew into it a couple of times, producing a thin, high-pitched sound, then threw it angrily into the snow, crushing it under his foot and setting off homewards, yawning. But all the animals in the Helsinki Zoo had heard it: from the shores of Suomenlinna, from the empty streets of Kruununhaka, from the observatory, perched on its hill, from as far away as the park at Korkeasaari. They pricked up their ears and craned their necks to listen. Blue foxes, zebras, guanacos, wolves, lynxes, owls, pandas, skunks, squirrels, Siberian tigers, deer, wild goats, reindeer, vultures and even the majestic arctic falcon moved off in the direction of the conference centre, summoned by the pipe of a man of the woods who knew how to talk to animals. The only ones who didn't answer the call were the lazy walruses, the hibernating bear, the wolverine and the baboons; their house had cooled down now that the glass had been smashed in, so they clambered up to the highest branch and formed a huddle, trying to keep warm. This time, none of the little ones dared to venture down on to the tractor wheel that hung there from its chain.

Ivan screwed up his courage and, following Urgel, proceeded guardedly in the direction of the city. He had no idea how he would get through that flickering inferno, but somehow it had to be got through, because all other ways to the sea were blocked. There in the open, far from Korkeasaari, the wind, encountering no obstacles, raised whirlwinds of snow which became tinged with yellow as they drifted citywards. The whole surface of the sea was crossed by its glancing breath, as though the ice were boiling magma on the point of exploding. The reindeer were advancing tentatively over the powdery terrain, but suddenly they pulled up short, pricked up their ears and dug their hooves firmly into the ice, refusing to go any further, sniffing the air, nostrils aquiver. Ivan looked around him, saw furtive shadows ahead of him. It was the wolves. Then he climbed off the sledge and gave eight long beats on his drum. Yellow eyes glinting, the dark shapes began to circle round him: tails between their legs, ready to leap, they followed one another closely. The last of the Vostyachs knelt down in front of them and beat out the slow compelling rhythm with which he had once called his people in the Byrranga Mountains. Little by little, he added his own voice to the drum's sombre roll, until it drove out the sound of the instrument altogether. Now it was just Ivan singing: his voice rang out like a drum-beat, a steady measure which, as it left his mouth, turned into words. '*Kyäyölöngkö!*' he thundered, pronouncing each letter clearly before he sent it forth into the air. This was the word uttered by Ululutoïon, the shaman with three shadows, who rises from the earth and disappears back into it. Ivan had learned it from his father, but this was the first time he had ever used it. On hearing it, the wolves lowered their heads and scattered, whimpering, dragging their snouts in the snow. Ivan walked towards the circle of footprints and saw a body lying on the ground, encased in ice. He went closer, touched the stiff limbs, which gave out a wooden sound as he moved them. In the dim starlight Ivan could not make out the face of the corpse that lay before him; the smell, however, was all too familiar. The Vostyach had smelt the sweetish, sweaty smell of a prostitute only once in his life – a few hours earlier, in a run-down room in Kallio; and it was a smell that would be with him always. He thought uneasily of the smooth skin which had made his blood run backwards through his veins, of the embrace in which his spirit had forsaken him. There must be something evil in this creature if she'd been capable of causing a Vostyach to take leave of his senses, dragging him into a world peopled only by empty images like those in dreams. But she could not be completely dead if she continued to follow him: perhaps any number of coloured fish were swimming beneath the ice, ready to shed their scales in order to bewitch him, the last of the Vostyachs. Even the wolves had given her a wide berth, a sure sign that evil spirits remained trapped within her flesh, nestling in her liver, ready to unleash disease and death in order to free themselves. She should be cooked, boiled until the flesh fell from her bones. Only that way would the spirits evaporate, get caught up again in the great breath which made the world go round.

But there was no time for that. They would have to be assuaged by the woman's burial; they would have to be plucked from the ice and driven skywards so that the breath of the universe could take them to itself again. Ivan loaded the body on to the sledge and set off for the beach at Tahvonlahti. He was thinking of cutting down a birch tree to make a catafalque on which to lay the body, but when he had almost reached the sea another dark shape caused the reindeer to stiffen. The Vostyach seized the axe and moved steadily towards it. This time too he recognized it by the smell. He knelt down and wept, inhaling the cheap scent of the only being in the world who had ever truly wished him well. Crouching beside the corpse, he drew it to his chest, as he had done so many years ago with his father. Twice, in the course of his harsh life, Ivan had cradled the lifeless body of the person who was dearest to him in his arms. He recognized the wave of grief which swept over him, as it had done all those years ago. He felt almost happy, because it was a familiar form of suffering and Ivan knew where it would strike hardest, where in his body it would lodge itself, sapping the strength from his legs, trapping his breath down in the pit of his stomach. Suddenly, he felt an age-old solitude descend upon him: that of his whole extinct people, of every Vostyach who had ever lost himself in the Siberian forests, who had ceased to speak and had gone to earth with the wolves, forgetting how to be a man. Now he himself no longer had anyone to speak to, no one with whom he could use the word describing something grey glimpsed vaguely running in the snow, or the colour of the birch trees when they are coming into leaf, or the smell of the lake as it unfreezes and gives off the fossil breath of hundred-year-old fish, the whistle of the wind as it blows in from the sea, dashing mountainous blocks of ice against the rocks.

Ivan cut down two young birch trees that were growing on the beach. He stripped them with the axe and fashioned them into eight white stakes, which he then laid out on the ice. He wove branches between them, and hoisted the bodies on to them, using the rope he'd taken from the storeroom in the zoo. He placed a stone on each woman's chest, together with the fragments of reindeer horn he'd brought with him in the sack. He decorated their hair with falcon feathers and covered their staring eyes with snow. Then he knelt before the catafalque and drummed out the song of sleep, accompanying it with a long lament, so that the great breath of the universe would slow down a little and take their lost spirits into its care.

Out of the wind in a phone box on Iso Roobertinkatu, Margareeta had made any number of calls to the police station on the other side of the road. Hyttynen was not answering. As they were going back into town, he had dumped her unceremoniously at the corner of Lönnrotinkatu. He wouldn't hear of going back later to Vasikkasaari, and he wasn't remotely interested in the story of the strange animals running about on the ice around the island. Helsingfors Idrottsföreningen Kamraterna was just a few points short of victory, and that did nothing to improve his temper.

'Listen, madam, you've already caused me to miss the hockey match and get frozen feet. Enough's enough! If you're looking for somebody to spend the night with, I suggest you try picking up someone in a nightclub. A new one has just opened at the end of the Bulevardi,' he had said to her dryly, pointing to the open door. Margareeta would have liked to ring her husband's bell just one last time, but she was exhausted. Her eyes were burning, her feet hurt and at each red light Hurmo would curl up on the ground and go to sleep. So she'd gone home, gulped down all the beer that was in the fridge and now she was drunk. She picked up the receiver without quite knowing who she was going to phone, then suddenly remembered Jarmo's answer phone and the newly rewound tape.

'I know you're listening, Jarmo. I know you're in there, in the dark. And I advise you not to throw away this tape: listen to it carefully, it may well be of use to you when we see each other again in court. I've been looking for you all day. I even went to Villa Suvetar, with the police. It was the only way I could be sure of getting the door opened. I know you've been there, no doubt accompanied by one of your 'women friends'. Isn't that what you called them? 'We share so many ideas, so many values, that sex is never going to rear its ugly head', you'd say to me whenever I dared to express puzzlement about the amount of time you spent with other women. I had to swallow lie upon lie. But you'd never done it at Villa Suvetar. You always spared the cottage at Vasikkasaari the mortifying spectacle of

your seductions, though I don't think that was out of respect for me. It was more likely the memory of your mother which prevented you from sullying the old holiday house where you had spent your childhood summers. So this is a sign that at last you feel truly free, of both me and your mother. Indeed, basically, for you we were one and the same: someone who would admire you, forgive you unconditionally, relish your successes as though they were our own. And whom you in your turn could cheat on. In your mother's case, this went no further than stealing a bit of loose change from her purse; in my case, it was my life you stole. Who did you take a sauna with in Villa Suvetar? With that student of yours with the big feet? Or with the Estonian lectrice? You disappoint me: the one this year is a real fright. And anyway, you'd have saved that sacred place for someone more useful to you. Some functionary at the Ministry of Education, perhaps? Or did you turn gay for one night in exchange for some important favour? Oh no, I see: that ugly great creature from the Vice-Chancellor's office who puts forward candidates for the Finnish Cross to the President of the Republic. After all, you'd stop at nothing, as we know.

But this is a strange night, Jarmo. Perhaps it's some unusual line up of the planets, or perhaps the cold has caused normally indissoluble chemical elements to separate. At all events, today I've seen things which have escaped me for fifteen years. This evening, the lights of Helsinki lit up the whole circuit of your vile doings. I made a bracing tour of all the places where you'd so gleefully deceived me, I visited the love nests I'd always known about but had never wanted to see, the sites of your finest lies, the pitiable ruins of a happiness which, though short-lived, had been very real. I happened to pass the local swimming-baths, and I remembered that short period when you used to go there regularly. After supper, every other day. Swimming was the only thing that helped your backache, you told me. I went on as far as Annankatu and walked past the block where the director of the Institute of Slavic Studies lives. Sinikka Hirvi, that was her name. And then I saw it all. It had taken me ten years. Now I know that you used to slip a bleach capsule into your bag together with your swimming suit and towel, and dissolve it in Sinikka Hirvi's bath tub so that you would come home smelling of chlorine, so as to convince me you'd really been at the pool. That was why those strange capsules had featured on the weekly shopping list for half a year – I had always wondered what you used them for. That was why, when I bought a mauve box, you smelt of lavender, and when I bought a yellow one, you smelt of citronella. I saw the faces of your lovers plastered over the walls of the city as though in a gallery. Even the ones I'd never met, even the journalist from the Helsingin Sanomat *you so wanted me to meet that Friday evening. I had to skip my piano lesson to join you at the Klaus Kinski. First you bedded them, then you introduced me to them. Why? Was it a way of ensuring my forgiveness? Or did you want to show them what you had given up in order to be with them? This afternoon, I went to look for you at the university. The windows in your office were open, the carpet was covered with snow and the floor was strewn with old papers and bits of glass. At first I was worried. I thought something awful might have happened and I went straight to the police station to report your disappearance. A policeman came with me to open your front door. But when I went into those rooms where you now live, without a single trace of your past life with me, as though I had never existed, I realized that I couldn't care less what had became of you. For all I care, you can sink into the ice in the sea off Helsinki or be burned alive in a car accident. It's all the same to me; I'd just like to be there when it happens. I want to cheer on the icy wave as it closes over your head and fills your mouth, to spur on the flames until they've charred you to a frizzle, like a fish on a spit, giving up on you only when they've reduced you to so much black mush stuck to the car seat. First, though, you've got to take Hurmo back; otherwise I'll flay him, stuff him and place him on your desk for you to gaze at until the last trump sounds!'*

Gripping the receiver so hard that it hurt, Margareeta felt herself positively salivating. She had so much more to say. Instead, she put the phone down and threw herself on to the bed, weeping, until at last she fell asleep in front of the blaring television.

Hurmo had taken refuge behind the armchair; as he well knew, when his mistress was in this kind of state he might well be in for a kicking. He hadn't even dared to go and stand beside his bowl, to let her know that he was hungry. At last, he too had fallen asleep, and was now snoring, a bit of carpet having fallen over his nose, hampering his breathing. But when the shut-down signal appeared on the screen, Margareeta had suddenly woken up, as though someone had called to her, or a hand shaken her. She had looked out of the window. The street was empty. The yellow lamplight made everything look weirdly two-dimensional, casting vague shadows over the windows of the parked cars. The ice which had again formed on the pavements gave off a gauzy light. In the distance, in the centre of town, a red shop sign was flickering on the top of a building, and from time to time the odd flash of red could be seen darting along the otherwise invisible threads of ice which meandered over the zinc roofs where the snow had melted. Margareeta looked at her watch: it was three o'clock, the eleventh of January was dawning. Now she was in the grip of a strange compulsion. She still had time to make that date somehow memorable. She poured herself a glass of vodka and put the bottle into the pocket of her windcheater. Dutch courage was what was needed. Then she went to dislodge Hurmo from behind his chair. Coming in, she hadn't even bothered to take off his lead. Now she gave it a firm tug, and the old dog whimpered as he slithered across the parquet. Dragging himself effortfully to his feet, he shook himself despondently and put out his tongue, rewarding his impatient mistress with a trusting look.

Four elks were galloping between the tramlines that ran along the Aleksanterinkatu, nimbly avoiding the lacerated bodies of several gazelles, over which a single vulture was doggedly hovering. A blue fox was sidling along in front of the windows of the Stockmann Supermarket, anxiously sniffing the air, then disappeared into the trees on the Esplanadi. Two pandas were loitering on the pavement opposite, uncertain where to go and scratching at the asphalt with their claws, hoping to find some earth. There was too much light around those parts, so they couldn't tell whether it was day or night. Three alpine goats were goading a lynx, which was following them at a distance, jaws agape, then disappeared behind the Swedish Theatre. Other dark shadows were snaking between the flashing traffic lights.

The Siberian tiger took the cathedral steps in four great bounds and felled one of the guanacos with a blow from its paw; it had followed them all the way from the Opera House. The other three lolloped off, quite unconcerned. The wounded animal did not make a sound; it turned away, then crumpled, belly up. The tiger sank its nose into the creature's stomach and dug its teeth into the soft flesh, shaking its prey as it did so; the guanaco was staring resolutely skywards, as though to distract attention from its entrails, which were spilling out on to the snow. Down in the square the wolves had pinioned two zebras and a mountain goat up against the colonnade and were preparing their attack, snarling the while; but while the terrorized zebras were huddling together, kicking out at the main door, the mountain goat was lowering its horns and leaping to and fro, fending off the assailants. The owl had come to rest on the statue of Czar Alexander II in the middle of the square, and was peering around in alarm, looking vainly for some quiet place to roost. Erect in the middle of the Unioninkatu, an old stag was casting a dispassionate glance at the scenes of mayhem going on around it, white breath issuing from its nostrils as it shook its thick complement of antlers. Seeing Ivan arriving at the far end of the street, it trotted away wearily. But the Vostyach carried on towards the Esplanadi, in search of some dark place where he could see the stars and get his bearings. He took his whip to his team of reindeer and disappeared into the trees. In the little wood at the foot of the Observatory the snow lay deep and undefiled, and the harbour lights were concealed behind a thick clump of pines. The benches looked like sleeping animals, and the swing in the middle of the rotunda resembled a sacred altar, its frame pointing towards the sky. Ivan tested the solidity of its posts, then looked upwards. There, at last, were the stars. The Vostyach stretched out on the ground and turned his head from side to side, inspecting the whole expanse of sky. He caught sight of Urgel, which seemed to be calling to him, waiting for him before going down. But Ivan knew he would have trouble negotiating that immense tangle of over-lit city streets. He took up the reins and got back on to the sledge. The little road through the park ran steeply down towards the sea, to the quay at Laivasillankatu.

Ivan had never seen a ship that size. Not even in the port

of Dudinka, where the soldiers had taken him one summer to load up the barges with coal for the foundry. Eight decks, a thousand blazing portholes, two huge smokestacks belching out black smoke. And loud, insistent noise, the smell of fuel, a line of lorries driving up on deck, clanging the while. Kneeling in the snow, the Vostyach gazed in enchantment at the Amorella, all lights ablaze, reflected in the channel of black water it had carved out for itself among the ice. He was exhausted. He hadn't eaten or slept for a whole day and night, he had spent the entire time wandering vainly around the gulf, trying to reach the forests. On his own he would never be able to find the tracks leading northwards, to get back to his people, to drag them out of their wild beasts' lairs and back into the sunlight. Moss would gather on his yurt, and finally it would collapse, to join all the other abandoned yurts that lay strewn throughout the woods. No Vostyach would ever again hear him singing in the tundra, in the Byrranga Mountains. Now that even Olga had abandoned him, what could he do on his own in the face of this hostile world? Where was that great and ancient tribe which understood his language and should have been there to welcome him in that alien land? Suddenly, Ivan felt that his life had really come to an end that night, so long ago, when his father had died in his arms. All those years spent in silence, breaking stones in the mine, were nothing but a poisonous excrescence which had bloomed forth from a body already dead. Like the nails on the hands of the convicts who had been crushed by falling rock, where the coal seam was at its deepest: over the long days it took for the skip from the barracks at Talnakh to reach the Byrranga Mountains to free those bodies, twisted white nails would continue to grow out of black hands. Escaping from the mine had served no purpose. Ivan should have died long ago, on that same night, he should have fallen down in the snow and heard and felt no more. But what about the bullet that was intended for him, where had that ended up? Why had none of the soldiers tried to aim at that little body running beside his father? Ivan was crying now, the tear drops freezing on his lashes. At that same moment, the child reappeared. At last he recognized himself: it was he who was the spirit that death had spurned, and which was now following him so doggedly. The Vostyach knew that spirits don't understand human speech; such was his dread that he nonetheless addressed a question to the shade standing before him:

'What is it you want?'

'To come with you.'

'Come with me where? I no longer have anywhere to go.'

'You told me you'd take me fishing on the lake, you said you'd teach me how to hunt coot in the marshes with my new bow,' the child protested mournfully.

'Tomorrow,' murmured Ivan, somewhat shamefaced. 'It's too late for that now.'

Ivan released the reindeer from the sledge and cracked the whip, urging them to move off. But they hadn't got anywhere to go to, any more than he had. They stayed in a huddle, a few steps away, tossing their heads. A lorry and trailer drew up on the quay and hooted loudly, frightening them off. Reversing on to the pontoon that led to the hold, it crushed Ivan's sledge beneath its spiked wheels and pushed it off the quay. The sledge floated briefly in the deep water before sinking into the foam whipped up by the ship's propellers. Ivan had crouched down by the wall of the harbour station. Through the bars of the gate he could see the sailors in the sentry box, the lighted pit of the hold where workers wearing big yellow gloves were pulling on ropes and chains. He looked at the guards in their red jackets, standing at the end of the gangway, and realized that he had no choice: he would have to give himself up. They might beat him, they might lock him up; they might bundle him on to a lorry and take him back to the mine, set him to breaking stones again. He should have died there twenty years ago, together with his father. It was wrong to try to avoid one's fate. Ivan felt in his pocket for his passport and set off for the gangway, utterly defeated.

The two Silja Line stewards conferred at length before allowing this strange passenger on board. He had a one-way ticket for Stockholm on the Meloodia, which had left some time ago, at 18.15. At that time of night the Amorella, en route from Tallinn to Stockholm, would not be picking up passengers, but only the odd lorry, and additional supplies of beer and fuel. But cabin 127 was empty, and in view of the fact that the stranger had a first-class ticket with meals, drinks and sauna thrown in, an exception could surely be made. In any case, neither steward felt like embarking on a lengthy argument with a Russian dressed in stinking skins. He had a ticket, he had a passport, and that was all that was required. They slipped a loop of coloured paper round his neck, gave him a leaflet about the duty-free goods obtainable on board and ushered him on to the upper deck, which was quiet and dimly lit. One of the stewards stopped to talk on the telephone, and Ivan took the opportunity to rub his numb hands and arms. Then a sleepy-looking stewardess appeared, to lead him along carpeted corridors, through saloons decorated with tropical plants and, finally, to his cabin. She turned on the light and then went out, shutting the door behind her. The Vostyach sat down on the edge of the bunk and waited for someone to come and question him, imagining the beating that would inevitably come his way: cracked ribs, no doubt, and blood-caked lips. The important thing was not to put up any resistance. The secret was to keep your head down and never look them in the eye.

Margareeta turned the key in the dashboard and blew on her hands, waiting for the engine to warm up. She felt for the bottle of vodka she had stuffed under the cushion of the seat beside her. Now safely in the car, she looked nervously up and down the street. Hurmo, sitting in the back, was also on tenterhooks, scrabbling around and whimpering. This wasn't a good time for a single woman to be wandering around alone near the station, let alone venturing out on to the frozen sea, but if Hyttynen wasn't going to help her, she would have to go back to Vasikkasaari on her own and have another look around the cottage. She was convinced that the key to the mystery lay somewhere on the island. The car made a creaking sound as it eased itself out of the ice in which it had been stuck, but the spiked wheels sank deeply into the snow. Margareeta drove carefully down to the goods yard. She had decided to make a thorough job of it. After all, she knew the state of the road, she'd been along it with Hyttynen just a few hours ago. But when she'd been through Tahvonlahti and found herself beside the sea, on the quay at Koirasaari, Margareeta took fright. She shone her headlights over the dark expanse that opened up before her, then took two gulps of vodka. But no, she simply didn't have the courage to drive out over that icy crust. She switched off the engine, leant her head wearily on the steering wheel and listened to Hurmo's laboured breathing. Then she got out of the car and walked to the end of the quay. Without really knowing what she was doing, she went down the steps and on to the beach. After a moment or two, Hurmo came bounding after her; he too was uneasy, and felt the need to keep within range of his mistress's reassuring scent. Margareeta looked towards Vasikkasaari, imagining her arrival in front of a darkened Villa Suvetar, and the strange animals that had been stalking around it. She ventured a few steps out on to the frozen sea, nervously feeling out the darker patches with her foot, exploring the projecting ridges hidden in the veins of shadow. Then, as though drawn by some irresistible attraction, she set out over the frozen waves towards the open sea, stopping every now and again to look behind her; then she would take a sip of vodka and carry on. Hurmo followed her, panting and sniffing out strange scents which distracted him from the smell of his mistress, causing him to make any number of pointless diversions over the ice. Margareeta wasn't sure if she was drunk or not. Her whole body felt strangely light. She didn't know whether she would ever get as far as Vasikkasaari, nor what she would find there if she did. Possibly nothing. But she felt that something was definitely coming to an end that night; even the stars in the sky were no longer quite the same. Some that she had never seen before were rising to the east, bringing a new wind with them, a new age in which life could begin afresh. The long illness that had been her marriage was being purged by the fever of the strange hours she was living through, which would leave her drained, but cured at last. But she would have to pass every station of that mysterious Calvary in order to ensure that the bitter memory of fifteen wasted years was well and truly wiped away. She might die in the attempt, she might fall through some crack in the ice or be torn limb from limb by the wild beasts she'd seen wandering the streets of Helsinki. It no longer mattered. She had to put herself through this ordeal in order to be cleansed.

Margareeta walked on, drunk and happy, raising her face to the cold wind now coming from the east. She felt she was being pursued by her wretched memories, by all those days she had wasted with that egotistical Jarmo, but that they would relinquish her somewhere out in the open sea, becoming transformed into so many monstrous icy hulks, never able to catch up with her again. She turned to look at Hurmo as he trudged behind her, and suddenly felt that he himself was the past from which she had to free herself. The fifteen years of her rotten marriage were all there, beneath his dirty coat and in his yellow eyes. She felt, even more strongly, that the new day must not dawn before she had rid herself of that loathsome creature. She walked on faster, clenching her fists in her pockets, seized with a sudden desire to sing. Then, equally suddenly, there in the open sea she found herself before a strange catafalque: taller than herself, it was made of birch branches and decorated with foliage and scraps of skin. When she saw what was on it she took a hasty step backwards, trembling with fear; then she ran off, unable even to utter a cry.

The chief of police himself had come to view the bodies of the two women found on the catafalque just off the island of Tahvonlahti. Seated in the back of the police van, Hyttynen was yawning as he sipped at the cup of coffee handed him by a colleague. His eyelids were swollen with tiredness and his windcheater was stained with blood. Recapturing all the animals which had escaped from the zoo had taken several hours. By the time the last Siberian tiger had been brought down by means of a dart containing a sleeping draught, the first trams were already running. People stared out of the windows in amazement at the sight of policemen going about the streets like hunters in the savanna, carrying mangled antelopes strung from a pole. Now dozens of police cars were flashing along the quays at Tahvonlahti, then setting off again for the city, sirens blaring. Margareeta, together with a nurse from the first-aid station, was waiting near the catafalque. She was still crying, and clearly very shaken, and the policeman who was questioning her was repeating his questions patiently, taking notes as he did so. Seated at her feet, whimpering anxiously from time to time, Hurmo appeared to be frowning, as though he too were trying to remember exactly what had happened. Dawn was now coming up, and the eastern sky was throbbing with pink light. The stars were drowning in the pale glow of morning, and long delicate lines of shadow were appearing on the snow. It was going to be a clear day. In the distance, Helsinki was coming back to life. Thick clouds of white smoke were rising from the buildings, one by one the blue streets were emerging from the dazzle of the lamplight; but banks of shadow still lingered above the sea, coming together towards the horizon to form one single leaden mass. In the harsh light of the floodlights, the faces of the corpses looked hacked clean of flesh, as gaunt as skulls; the women had feathers in their hair, and coloured stones had been laid on their chests. A policeman removed a bit of ice from one of Olga's eyes, covered up Katia's naked thighs and nodded towards the waiting ambulance. Two nurses came forward with stretchers. They spread red and yellow ribbons around the catafalque, then set up pickets with numbered pennants on the ice. One policeman was busy taking measurements, while others swept away the snow. Comment was offered in hushed tones. Flashbulbs went off, a radio croaked from a distant car. Engines were started, and the chief of police went back to the dark car from which he had emerged, chilled to the bone. Nobody paid any attention to Hurmo, who had approached the bodies and was now sniffing at them cautiously. Then he let out a sudden bark and started scratching away at Olga's body, seeming to rummage through her clothing. The chief of police was called back, and the floodlights were again trained on to the bodies. Hurmo was jumping around, barking playfully: now he was straddling the body, now throwing himself against it, tail wagging furiously, shaking his head from side to side as he tugged doggedly at a scrap of fabric protruding from her jacket. A policeman came forward and freed a pair of blue silk men's pyjamas from the ice. Through her tears, Margareeta recognized the monogram J. A. embroidered on the pocket. This was the last birthday gift she'd given him: a special offer from the great firm of Marimekko.

Ivan woke up in a sweat. He sat up in his bunk not knowing where he was, and gazed around him in bewilderment at the dimly-lit cabin. He was hungry and thirsty. He felt around on the shelves, in the drawers of the bedside locker, among the covers. He pulled on a handle and found himself faced by a row of bottles; there were also bars of chocolate and packets of crisps and nuts. He ate everything in sight, sampled each of the bottles and polished off the one with the blue label with the figure of a stag. He liked the sweet, fresh flavour: it reminded him of berries. His head was spinning, and his limbs, tense for so long with weariness and fear, were now at last relaxing. He undid his leather jacket and took it off. Now he was stripped to the waist, but the little low room was horribly stuffy, and he needed air. He picked up his sack, slung his drum round his neck and went out into the corridor. He came to a gangway with a glassed-in parapet, overlooking a thronged saloon. Dazzlingly elaborate chandeliers cast light on men with polished shoes, sinking their moustaches into tankards of beer and clutching half-naked women clasping glasses of brightly coloured liquid. A sweet scent hovered over everything, not unlike the one that pervaded the refectory in the mine on feast days, when lorry-loads of soldiers would come over from the barracks, singing and waving red flags. Beyond the glass door there was a wider corridor, walled with glass and mirrors. This led into another saloon, where the light came from panels set into the floor, causing Ivan to proceed with caution. The sight of a group of guards, in red jackets and white gloves, caused him to panic, but they simply smiled at him and moved off in the wake of the noisy throng. A staircase with small lamps on the handrail led up to a round dance-floor, roofed by a black dome studded with little lights, like a night sky but with a tangle of wires and steel pipes hanging down from it. Beyond the dance floor was a raised platform on which Ivan could make out two drums similar to his own, as well as a much larger one, standing on a tripod, its skin kept taut by four iron pegs. People were swarming into the saloon and sitting down on the soft carpet which covered the staircase steps. Ivan did the same, partly because his head was swimming and his vision was becoming blurred. The lights went out, and a spotlight picked out four figures seated on the stage, dressed in multi-coloured fabrics and strange pointed hats. Enthralled, Ivan gazed at the cymbals flashing in the darkness, listened to the electric guitars spitting out volleys of metallic sound worthy of submachine-guns. He listened enchanted as the saxophone let out its solitary wail, sending out flashes which lit up the faces of the audience. But when the awesome wave of sound of the big drum set the air throbbing, and the sound of deep singing rose up from the stage, Ivan leapt to his feet. That was his music! That was the rhythm the hunters of Tajmyr beat out on their drums to lure the bears out of their dens! Without thinking, without realizing he was doing so, the Vostyach began to dance, stamping his right foot twice, his left three times, then both feet together, arms raised. He let go of his sack and raised his drum to his chest; then he too started playing the song of the maddened bear. The spotlight swerved away from the stage and settled on to him. The musicians abandoned their scores and matched their rhythm to his own demonic beat, while the audience clapped

Diego Marani

enthusiastically, thinking that the dishevelled individual in the tattered skins was a member of the Estonian folk group 'Neli Sardelli' performing for them there that evening.

When Ivan stopped playing, panting and sweating, to mad applause, the musicians rushed to cluster around him and bear him off with them on to the stage, putting microphones, kettledrums, hunting horns and a whole range of other drums before him. But Ivan batted them all away with a sweep of his hand, clutching his drum of reindeer skin more closely to his chest. He sighed deeply, narrowed his eyes and, with the tips of his fingers, drummed out the beat that told of the bear's dash through the trees; then, with his knuckles, he played out its roar; with the flat of his hand he played its flight, and, with a grazing motion, he imitated the sound of the hunters' arrows as they whistled through the air, piercing the bear's coat with a moist thwack. When at last he laid them, open, down on the hard leather, his hands were burning, throbbing like wounds. He got down on his knees, lowered his chin and stayed there for several minutes, motionless. The audience stared at him with bated breath. Now came the magic song for warding off the devil, who was preparing to pounce once the bear's spirit left his body. Ivan inhaled as deeply as he could; he needed all the breath he could muster for this song.

Uutta murha ristirimme
Pehkavalla pokevemme
Ulitalla tohkevasti
Pikku ranta vikevasti

Naike viike tukavanne
Ei se loutta polevanne
Namma tilla vanta rokka

149

Simme karatali ehka

Toise timmo rantaseli
Eika poro muisteseli
Murha tavon eli koska
Riitta sahko pulliselkska

Uutta murha ristirimme
Pehkavalla pokevemme
Ulitalla tohkevasti
Pikku ranta vikevasti

Ivan was beating time with his feet, smothering the words of his song within his throat so that they would raise no echo; that was what the hunters of Tajmyr had done. His song rose through the room like smoke, cloaked in hoarse warmth. Listening to those wild shouts no one had ever heard before, the audience was ecstatic, and began to sway along with the rhythm. As though wearing a succession of ever-changing masks, the Vostyach's twisted his face into a thousand different grimaces as he forced the breath up from his belly and turned it into song. It was not just his voice that sang, but his eyes, his nose, his hands, his legs, his arching back, his whole body. Slowly, the people around him started repeating the odd word, then a verse, then the whole song. In the freezing night, the whole Baltic echoed with the song of the men of the tundra which had come down from the distant peaks of the Byrranga Mountains to the land of the thousand lakes.

Uutta murha ristirimme
Pehkavalla pokevemme

150

Ulitalla tohkevasti
Pikku ranta vikevasti

bellowed the drunken Finnish tourists at the tops of their voices, not understanding a word of what they were saying, raising their tankards with one hand and using the other to touch up their partners, themselves scarlet in the face from alcohol and the excitement of that unprecedented spectacle. None of them realized that what they were singing was in fact Vostyach, the unknown ancient language which linked them to the American Indians. None of them knew that the lateral fricative with labiovelar overlay was once more returning to its natural home, their very own mouths, and that thousands of miles away, across the ocean, deep within the Canadian forests, seated in a circle around their coloured totems on their reservations, the Algonquin Indians pronounced it in exactly the same way in their songs invoking the spirits of their ancestors. Yet, strangely, on the Aland Islands which were now streaming past them on the other side of the glass, the elk now raised their heads, the owls opened their eyes, the hares pricked up their eyes in their dens. Salmon, herring and whitefish, their bellies streaked with mauve, rose to the surface from the frozen depths and slithered silently behind the Amorella as she picked her way between the shattered ice floes heading for Stockholm, all lights ablaze.

The professor paused: he had already been speaking for twenty minutes. He poured himself a glass of water before carrying on, and the sound rang out like a cataract in the total silence of the lecture hall. He had now almost reached the end of his speech, but no one had laughed or clapped at the points where his secretary had put the asterisks. Cowed by Aurtova's steady glare, by his wooden movements and dogmatic tone, the audience had listened to him in subdued silence, barely risking a cough, obscurely convinced that something momentous was about to happen. His expression invisible behind his thick glasses, rather than taking notes in preparation for some poisonous riposte, even Juknov was peering around as though seeking help. In the brief pause files rustled, chairs creaked, noses were blown; in their booths, the interpreters made use of the short interruption to consult each other about some problem word. But when Aurtova put down his glass and turned over the last sheet of his speech, silence reigned once more.

'I would like to conclude with a reflection which may perhaps seem harsh, but which is today more relevant than ever: I would like to launch an appeal which may affront the more tender-hearted among you, but which I nonetheless hope will prick the consciences of those who have our language and our culture truly at heart.

In this age of stagnation and decline, certain sated and jaded nations have squeezed themselves into history, only to find they can't get out. They clog up the course of events, wallowing in their decadence. Like some monstrous misshapen tumour, they are sprouting from the very thing which throttles them. In the normal course of events it would take centuries before they were digested, before their flesh dissolved, hardened as it is by its thousand-year acquaintanceship with evil. But their incurable corruption produces recurrent flare-ups of infection in which thousands of human beings are annihilated. How many more gulags, how much more ethnic cleansing will it take before humanity is purged of that toxic pustule, the Slavs? For how long will man's progress towards all that is good continue to be hampered by these corrupt and backward nations, scions of a primitive world that is no more? All forms of life, each man, each plant, each animal, each stone, strain inexorably to move on from the purely material, to march towards the perfection which will link them once more to God. But the dinosaurs of our time refuse to die, and their interminable death throes oblige the rest of humanity to linger on in a world of evil. Their very language has turned against them: it no longer stills incomprehension but foments it, and, when words have become irretrievably snarled up, a language will subdivide and move ever further away from its original meaning, indeed from any meaning. Then debate and even invective become vain, and we are left with just yes and no, and black and white. This spiral of destruction spawns monstrous languages, designed to conceal, to deceive, to erect a barrier between words which were once held in common, to give them double meanings, so that even the most humdrum of phrases – "Hallo, who's speaking?" for example – may trigger off a war. In the new world we're all waiting for, a drastic new morality will be needed, one which will ensure the suicide of any distinctive group when it becomes useless or threatening to the rest of humankind. People who can no longer be understood should have the humility to change languages, seeking continued existence in the freshness of another tongue, cleansing themselves through some salutary cultural transfusion which puts new sap in their veins, and infuses new grace into their customs.

It was the Greeks who fostered the slippery notion of democracy, the tortuous concept of the state, the unnatural condition of living penned up within city walls. This was the model adopted by continental Europe, which further elaborated the concept of creeping, all-pervasive governance and cherished the teeming cesspit of the city and the myth of the public institution. But what is an institution? It is an empty building where no one lives, it is faceless and anonymous, even its telephones remain unanswered. All these ideas are alien to Finnish culture. For us, the village is the centre of all things, the institution is a living being, which sits itself down and drinks beside us, whose every secret we are privy to, which bares its all to us openly in the sauna. So it is to the village that we must return and, by founding one after another, repopulate the land we have abandoned, bringing back the music of our language into forests that have too long been silent, intimidated by the Slavic bark. This is how we will escape the steam-roller of the great western democracies and their blackmailing call for enforced assimilation. But we must do more besides, combining renewed cultural expansionism with firm yet passive resistance. Now I shall explain how this might be done.

Over these last years we have at last been able to take stock of the state of the various Finno-Ugric languages, and have found them to be in rude health and consistent growth, much more so than their past history might suggest. Driven by enemy peoples out of their first homelands into the Siberian tundra at the edge of the occupied world, forced to live in climatic conditions which put their very existence in jeopardy, the Finnish peoples survived centuries of persecution, and indeed of genocide during the dark Soviet era. Besieged by the hostile tide of Slavs, our peoples resisted cultural assimilation, keeping the memory of their mother tongue alive to the point that it may now at last be reborn. Suddenly a mood of brotherhood is stirring once again, one which we thought had been put out, but which is now making itself felt from the Urals to the Atlantic, from Mordvia to Karelia, from Ingria to Hungary, over an area the size of Western Europe. All in *all, what saved our peoples from Russianization and linguistic annihilation was not just their intrinsic physical robustness, their dogged hold on life, their fighting spirit, but sheer ignorance. It was our ignorance of the Russian language, our refusal to learn it and to surrender to the dominant culture, which enabled our peoples to survive linguistically. If today Nenets, Ngnasan, Mordvin, Vogul and Votic are still spoken, it is because they have been protected by their speakers' ignorance. Instead of learning Russian and improving their social condition by moving into the great industrial centres or emigrating to more prosperous areas, the Finnish peoples preferred to barricade themselves behind their own language, thus remaining impervious to Russianization.*

And this should serve us as an example. In the world of mass culture, where the weaker languages are threatened by a new linguistic colonialism which stifles minority cultures, only ignorance can protect us from extinction. My call to the new generations, here as in the former Soviet Republics of Finnish stock, is therefore this: cherish ignorance, do not study the language of the foreigner, but force him to learn your own! Since he cannot take on the world's linguistic colossi on equal terms, all that the speaker of a Finnic language can do is to adopt an attitude of resolute, dumb ignorance, the very one which has enabled him to survive intact over so many centuries. Ignorance will be our strength, our breast plate, and it will sabotage linguistic imperialism until it is no more. We must never forget that expansion always saps the strength, and that the day will inevitably come when the dominant languages crumble away. Too far from their meanings, like an advance guard too far from their supply lines, such foreign words as are still trickling into the Finnic languages will be swallowed up by the very tongues which they themselves were destined to stifle; their sounds and phonemes will be cast out, their double

*consonants will fall away, their vowels will broaden out and
the language of true men will be reborn. Who today recognizes
the Indo-European roots of our familiar* ranta *or* pullo *or*
kaupunki? *Yet these were originally Germanic words, which
were brought into Finland with domination in mind. But the
Finnic languages gobbled them up, turned "strand", "bottle"
and "kaufpunkt" into something of their own, stripping away
the undesirable sounds which our mouths found hard to
pronounce, giving new strength to tainted vowels and merging
three untidy palatals into a single velar, thereby creating new
and solid words, destined to last forever.*

*So, on this solemn occasion, I am taking advantage of this
celebration of our languages to express the hope that, in fifty
years times, no one between the Gulf of Bothnia and the White
Sea will know one single word of English or of Russian, and
that the vocalic harmony of the Finno-Ugric languages will
ring out loud and clear, dense and compact as our own forests.
Long live Finland! Long live ignorance!'*

Such desultory applause as Aurtova's speech elicited was
short-lived; the packed lecture hall seemed in the grip of some
nameless dread. The eyes of most of the audience were no
longer on the speaker's platform, bedecked with flowers and
flags, but on the group of policemen advancing warily from
the back of the hall, leaving damp footprints on the linoleum.
Their leader stood stiffly at the foot of the dais, waiting for
the professor to descend to his own level, then asked him
demurely for his personal details, reading out every word from
the identity card the great man coolly handed him. Then, in a
voice touched with regret, he uttered the indictment:

'Professor Jarmo Aurtova, I declare you under arrest for the murder of Olga Pavlovna and Katia Rekhsadze'.

Staring into the middle distance, Aurtova held out his wrists to receive the handcuffs and followed the police without a word. He walked through the hall with a martial step, holding his head high in the midst of the crowd which drew aside to let him pass. The photographers who were awaiting him in the entrance hall seemed cowed by his haughty demeanour, scarcely able to perform their function: the face they saw before them, which would stare forth from the crime pages of the *Helsingin Sanomat*, was not that of a murderer, but of a hero, fit for some monument to the fallen, some commemorative medal, a thousand-mark banknote. Aurtova did not see the rows of blank faces in front of him; his impassive gaze was not on the hall around him, nor on the buildings of the city that could be glimpsed beyond the great glass door, nor even on the hazy horizon beyond. He was gazing into distances yet more remote, beyond the sky, beyond time itself. He was staring, mesmerized, into the spinning maelstrom of the future as it swallowed centuries, peoples, seas and mountains. The Vostyachs' yurts were ripped to tatters as they were sucked into the eye of that mighty cyclone, along with Pecheneg horsemen, Viking hordes, Cossack horses, Swedish galleons. Outside, on the quay in front of the conference centre where the crowd had gathered to observe the scene, the professor did not deign to cast even the briefest of glances at his ex-wife, or at poor Hurmo, who was whimpering and straining on the leash to run to greet his master. He turned his back on the two figures who were waiting for him in the snow; for one brief moment he looked out to sea, breathed in a deep lungful of sea air and got into the police van, doing up the top button of his coat as he did so.

While he was being driven across the city on his way to

the prison at Valilla, Professor Aurtova still had no idea who or what it was that had given him away. Nor did he care. The Director of the Institute of Finno-Ugric languages at the University of Helsinki had no regrets, indeed he was proud of what he had done. He lifted his head and thrust out his chest as he drove past the white faculty colonnade.

Even when he learned that it was his pyjamas that had betrayed him, he didn't bat an eyelid. He didn't realize that Olga had put them on before losing consciousness and that he, fumbling around in the dark, had mistaken them for her silk blouse. As to the mysterious catafalque the papers talked of in the days that followed, Aurtova was certain that it was the work of Pecheneg horsemen, and he was surprised that no one seemed interested in tracking them down. Why was no one pursuing them to the Estonian coast; burning down their villages, running their swords through their children's heads and stringing them up from the trees, as those bloodthirsty barbarians themselves had done with the Finns? Pecheneg children should be tracked down and impaled in full view of their fathers, so that no Pecheneg would dare ever again to raise a sword against the Finnish peoples. It did not even enter the professor's head that it had been Ivan who had built that gruesome monument, that he had not in fact embarked for Sweden but was still wandering the streets of Helsinki. The Vostyach must disappear from the face of the earth, along with all his kind. In the nightmare visions into which he was ever more often plunged, Aurtova imagined Ivan roaming the streets of Stockholm, chased off like a tramp, pursued like a thief, disease-ridden in some poorhouse. He dreamed that he had become a drug addict, an alcoholic, rotting away in a Swedish prison, or dead in some harbour brawl, his body thrown into the sea. Festering in the dark waters of the port of

Stockholm, his body would soon have turned to mud, food for the fish, a fossil shell, empty and silent, sent rolling to and fro by the cold currents on the ocean floor.

Seated on a bench in his prison cell, hands in his lap and knees together, as though he were in church, Aurtova would look through the bars on the narrow windows, seeing the streets and squares of his city, imagining the great rooms of his exclusive apartment. He knew he wouldn't be seeing any of them again for quite some time. But, with a bit of luck, he might be out in time for he XXIVth Congress of Finno-Ugric languages, which was to be held in Budapest. And what are fifteen years in the life of a language?

Hurmo flicked the foam from his muzzle and dug in his claws, thoroughly unwilling to be immersed in that soapy water. But Margareeta took him lovingly in her arms, all fat and shapeless as he was, and laid him delicately down amidst the bubbles. At first he stiffened, lowered his ears and let out a powerful howl. Then, under the caresses of his mistress, he relaxed, folded his paws and curled up in the warm water. He even allowed his stomach to be brushed, put up with the jet of water trained on his chest, staring resignedly at his soaking fur. He shook himself with relief into the towel in which Margareeta had wrapped him, proffering each paw in turn to have it dried. Lastly, he opened an obedient mouth and swallowed the worming pill. That was how it was every Sunday, and by now Hurmo was used to it. He had become used to everything; except for his new name.

'You'll never see your master again,' Margareeta had told him one summer evening as she came into the house and threw herself wearily on to the bed. She had taken off her high-heeled shoes and had spent a few moments staring at the ceiling while Hurmo panted suspiciously on his little armchair.

'Well, if fate has decreed that you and I should be together, we might as well resign ourselves, don't you agree?' she had added, getting up to give him a stroke, the first he'd had since the divorce. He wagged his tail timidly, but kept his distance.

'Meanwhile, the first thing we have to do is to change your name, because Hurmo is a dog's name, and you're a bitch. From now on you'll be called Kukka, do you understand? And my word, Kukka, what a beauty you're going to be!'

So Hurmo had become Kukka, and he no longer slept on the little armchair in the bedroom, which was filthy by now, but under the kitchen window in a brand-new basket lined with flowered material. He had his food in a pink bowl under the sink, and a new real leather collar with a little bell, which in fact made him feel a bit like a cat, but on the other hand it also gave him a touch of pedigree. But when Margareeta took him for walks in the Observatory Gardens, he never responded to his new name. That was the only, minor disappointment he continued to cause his mistress.

From his position in the wooden dock in the lawcourt, Professor Aurtova had answered all the Public Prosecutor's questions with a smile, describing everything that had happened on that far-off night of the ninth of January for the umpteenth time to a courtroom criss-crossed by gilded rays of dusty sunlight. He had confirmed that it was he and only he who had dragged the bodies of both women into the frozen sea where they would meet their deaths, after having made them drunk and drugged them with sleeping pills. He explained that he had lured them to the cottage with promises of generous financial rewards if they lent themselves to his secret sexual fantasies. At that point the members of the jury had coughed nervously in their seats, and a shocked murmur had gone up from the public, losing itself in the austere vaults above. The judge had politely called for silence and blushingly begun to leaf through his sheaf of papers, before inquiring somewhat bashfully about the precise nature of such fantasies. Then the professor had again assumed the distant, vacant look which the prison doctors had noted with concern some days previously, when Aurtova had been brought into the infirmary, bound to a stretcher completely naked. Then the Public Prosecutor returned to his charge, wanting to know how the professor had managed to construct the strange catafalque on which he had laid the bodies, with all those peculiar scraps of leather and feathers and plaited hair. He had approached the accused with a faintly threatening air, ordering him to explain the hidden meaning of that diabolical construction. Aurtova had explained to him, precisely and patiently, how he had found the timber in the woods on the nearby islands, and cut the trees down with his axe. He had used his rope to bind the trunks to the tow coupling on his car and pulled them into the sea, where he had built the catafalque. As to its meaning, here the professor had shaken his head, and his eyes had suddenly gone blank: now they were fixed on the throngs of Pechenegs pressed up against the lowering wind-scoured sky, riding across the steppe, brandishing the translucent skins of their flayed enemies from the tips of their lances like so many paper banners, like kites in human form. The lawyers had looked at each other, shrugging their shoulders. In the public gallery, the women had pressed their knees together in disapproval, and the men sighed heavily, crossing their arms. The judge had risen to his feet and the members of the jury had trooped out of the courtroom in an orderly fashion.

Over the days which followed, Professor Aurtova underwent further psychiatric tests and was diagnosed as suffering from schizophrenia, a danger to himself and others. The windows of the mental hospital in which he was confined looked out on to a wood, not far from the sea: in the autumn the leaves briefly took on a variety of lovely hues, and when the leaves fell there was a distant view of the seashore, the sea forever grey and dark between the white trunks of the birch trees.

The manager was a short, fat man who looked very like the doctor in the mine. Ivan was not sure what was wanted of him, but he had at least understood that this strange smartly turned-out figure was pleased to see him play the drum and dance with the other musicians on the stage in the big saloon with the flashing floor. Scarcely a week had gone by since Ivan had embarked on his improvised number, but already everyone on board the Amorella was singing his songs: the waiters while they were serving at the bar, the ship boys as they mopped the kitchen floors, the officers when they were playing cards on the bridge; even the seven Somalis who worked cooped up in the oily heat of the engine-room would burst cheerily into *Uutta murha ristirimme* as though it were a shepherd's song from Ogaden. The ships' turbines throbbed to the rhythm of Ivan's drum, the foghorn played along in time to it and the propellers danced to the beat of the wild music as they turned in the water. Thus the Samoyedic language of the Vostyachs, which scholars believed extinct, could truly be said to be alive and flourishing from the hold to the smart upper deck, from stem to stern, of one large ship in the middle of the Baltic Sea. The weary, happy tourists who poured off the Amorella at the end of the cruise, laden with souvenirs and liquor bottles, all went home singing that irresistible refrain, those perfect, rounded sounds which left the mouth sated and the heart at rest. So, throughout Finland, in showers, on skis, in sawmills, in workshops, queuing along the ring road around Espoo or in the grey factories of Pasil, Vostyach was coming back to life among the people to whom it had one day belonged. In the forests the wood grouse raised their crests, the bears roared as they reared up on their hind legs and the lemmings crowded together around the banks of the lakes to hear the sound of their ancient name which no one had uttered for years.

When Ivan went back into the changing room after his performance, the short fat man came after him to accompany him, smiling, to the restaurant on the upper deck, and had him served at a table with a white cloth, right by the window, with a view of the sea. Ivan had never seen it so brightly lit up by the moon. He liked it on that ship, together with his new friends from the 'Neli Sardelli' folk group, even if he had difficulty in communicating with them, and sometimes felt that they were teasing him, laughing and pulling wry faces; but then they would slap him on the back, and he knew that there was no malice in what they did. He could see in their eyes that they were fond of him, and when the ship docked at Stockholm or Marieham they would never leave him on his own. They took him around with them to the beer houses, to the cinema, or window-shopping. The only place he refused to go to was the striptease joints: he was afraid of women baring swollen breasts and hard buttocks in the glare of psychedelic lighting. They reminded him of the black shape with its smell of internal organs which had driven him beside himself that distant winter morning. So he would stay outside, seated in some bar where his friends would buy him crisps and beer, signalling to the barman to keep an eye on him. They too had begun to refer to him as 'Vostyach', because Ivan had said the word a thousand times to explain who he was and where he came from. But the Estonian musicians knew nothing of the Vostyachs, they had never been hunting in the tundra, and Ivan was unable to explain to them where the Byrranga Mountains were. On summer nights, when they stayed up on deck, looking at the white sky, Ivan would indicate the distant point in the middle of the sea where Urgel set; but no one knew what he meant. They would give him another bottle of beer and sit him down on a deckchair, hoping he'd forget and quieten down.

Sometimes his people had appeared to him in dreams: Korak, Haino, old Taypok. He'd seen his father coming towards him over the ice, smiling, with a big fish hanging from the bait. Then he had awoken with a start, remembering the wolves which howled in the forest in Tamjyr, unable to become men again. But all that was now too far away, and Ivan wanted to forget about it. He no longer wanted to think about the mine or to meet the child who had never died, and if, on lonely nights, he sometimes felt like weeping, it was only for the fair-haired woman who had been fond of him. The gate of memory was open for her alone. In the evening, before falling asleep, he found himself repeating the words he had spoken for her to capture in the little black box which talked on its own. He remembered them all, and each one of them brought back images of those happy days. He remembered the inn, the tarred roofs of the houses in the village of the turnip-growers, his favourite trees, the fair-haired woman who smiled as she listened to him, and the rounded hills of the Byrranga Mountains in the distance, the deer's head and the two protruding points like hares' ears. He remembered the time in the Byrranga Mountains when each name adhered magically to the thing to which it belonged, and the tundra rang with the mighty Vostyach language; he remembered the men who could talk with wolves, who knew the name of the black fish which lived in the mud of the arctic lakes, of the fleshy moss which bloomed in high summer just for one day, purpling the rocks above the Tamjyr Peninsula. He remembered the men who had found the way out of the dark forest to another world, but never the way back.

All this happened many years ago. Now Professor Aurtova no longer sees Pecheneg and Tartar horsemen riding over the ceiling of his white-painted cell. He has been given permission to have a small bookshelf beside his bed, and a desk beneath the window. He has had the university doorman send him his precious edition of Paavo Kurjensaari's *Encyclopedia of Finno-Ugric Languages*, the big Finnish dictionary edited by Jukka Svinhufvud and Heino Virkunen and some outdated handbooks of Uralic Philology. He spends his days declining irregular nouns and reconstructing the etymology of old words no longer mentioned in the dictionaries. He has pinned up the postcards which the doorman sends him from his holidays on the wall above his desk. He keeps a careful daily diary, and the speech he intends to give at the XXIVth Congress of Finno-Ugric languages, the one to be held in Budapest, is already stowed away in the drawer of his bedside table. Hurmo now rests under a birch tree in a wood outside Helsinki, although the wooden board nailed into the bark, its pink paint already peeling off, refers to him as Kukka. Margareeta has sold her Helsinki apartment and has gone to live with her sister in Kemi, where the sea always freezes over in winter in the course of a single night, so that the melancholy lilt of the last autumn waves remains before your eyes until the following spring.

On a cruise ship plying the Baltic from Helsinki to Stockholm, the last of the Vostyachs earns his living by performing with the Estonian folk group 'Neli Sardelli'. He plays a drum made of reindeer skin, singing the ancient songs of a mysterious language which makes your hair stand up on end; which makes you want to pray.

New Finnish Grammar - Diego Marani

New Finnish Grammar won three literary prizes in Italy: Premio Grinzane Cavour, Premio Ostia Mare and Premio Giuseppe Desi and has received critical acclaim across Europe. It has been shortlisted for The Independent Foreign Fiction Award 2012.

"A wounded sailor is found on a Trieste quay — amnesiac, unable to speak and with nothing to identify him except a name tag pointing to Finnish origins. A passing doctor resolves to teach him Finnish to restore his memory and rebuild his identity. Charming and beguiling."
Books of the Year in *The Financial Times*

"...this is an extraordinary book, as good as Michael Ondaatje's *The English Patient* and with a similar mystery at its heart."
Cressida Connolly in *The Spectator's Books of the Year*

"...an entrancing, disturbing exploration of the limits of speech and self." Boyd Tonkin in *The Independent*

"Beautifully written and translated, and beautifully original." Kate Saunders in *The Times*

"It was, naturally, the flatness of the title that attracted me: it bespoke, in its quiet confidence, a deep, rich and eventful inner life. And besides, I have some inkling of what Finnish grammar is like: fiendishly complex, basically, and related to no other languages on earth save Hungarian and Estonian. Deep and rich, did I say? That isn't the half of it. I can't remember when I read a more extraordinary novel, or when I was last so strongly tempted to use the word 'genius' of its author." Nick Lezard's Choice in *The Guardian*